**There was** ~~a~~ eyes. **"What is the last thing you remember?"**

The busy restaurant floated in her vision again. Her mother. Georgios. Alexis.

"They want me to marry you," she blurted out, the words forming a beat before the memory. She met Thanasis's stare again. "My family want me to marry you to save Tsaliki Shipping."

His green eyes didn't blink. "What else? What else do you remember?"

She shook her head in fear and frustration. "Nothing. There's nothing else."

The next pause stretched for an age. When he finally spoke, Thanasis's voice had lost the taut edge she'd only been barely aware it contained. "Lucie, look at your wedding finger."

Her heart seemed to go into stasis as she unclenched her hand and carefully lifted it, mindful of the medical line running into it. And then every atom in her body contracted with shock to see the sparkling diamond ring on her finger.

"This isn't possible," Lucie whispered.

"You agreed to marry me," he said quietly. "Our wedding is in nine days."

*A brand-new enthralling Harlequin Presents duet from Michelle Smart.*

# Greek Rivals

*Two opposing families... Two forbidden passions?*

Thanasis Antoniadis and Alexis Tsaliki are fierce competitors. The feud between their families has been raging in Greece for decades—and it's driving both their billion-euro shipping empires into the ground. They need to find a way to save their families' fortunes and put an end to this conflict. So falling for women who are their sworn enemies is the last thing either of them needs...

Thanasis agrees to marry Lucie, Alexis's stepsister, to end the rumors of hostility. When an accident leaves Lucie with no memory of their convenient engagement, Thanasis has no choice but to keep up the fiancée facade. And to keep his distance from the enemy he's dangerously tempted by!

Read Thanasis and Lucie's story in
*Forgotten Greek Proposal*

Lydia Antoniadis is the last woman Alexis should be sharing a sizzling night with. No one is more off-limits than his rival's sister! And neither could have anticipated that their recklessly passionate encounter would have such shocking and life-changing consequences...

Discover Alexis and Lydia's story,
coming soon!

# FORGOTTEN GREEK PROPOSAL

## MICHELLE SMART

**PRESENTS**

**Harlequin®**
**PRESENTS™**

Recycling programs for this product may not exist in your area.

ISBN-13: 978-1-335-93984-5

Forgotten Greek Proposal

Copyright © 2025 by Michelle Smart

For questions and comments about the quality of this book, please contact us at CustomerService@Harlequin.com.

TM and ® are trademarks of Harlequin Enterprises ULC.

Harlequin Enterprises ULC
22 Adelaide St. West, 41st Floor
Toronto, Ontario M5H 4E3, Canada
www.Harlequin.com

MIX
Paper | Supporting responsible forestry
FSC® C021394

**Printed in Lithuania**

**Michelle Smart**'s love affair with books started when she was a baby and would cuddle them in her cot. A voracious reader of all genres, she found her love of romance established when she stumbled across her first Harlequin book at the age of twelve. She's been reading them—and writing them—ever since. Michelle lives in Northamptonshire, England, with her husband and two young smarties.

## Books by Michelle Smart

### Harlequin Presents

*Innocent's Wedding Day with the Italian*
*Christmas Baby with Her Ultra-Rich Boss*
*Cinderella's One-Night Baby*
*Resisting the Bossy Billionaire*
*Spaniard's Shock Heirs*

### Scandalous Royal Weddings

*Crowning His Kidnapped Princess*
*Pregnant Innocent Behind the Veil*
*Rules of Their Royal Wedding Night*

### A Billion-Dollar Revenge

*Bound by the Italian's "I Do"*

### The Greek Groom Swap

*The Forbidden Greek*

### The Diamond Club

*Heir Ultimatum*

Visit the Author Profile page
at Harlequin.com for more titles.

# CHAPTER ONE

THE PAIN THAT shot through Lucie Burton's eyes when she peered between her lids was so great it momentarily distracted her from the pneumatic drill boring into her head. It also stopped her registering the man sitting beside her, engrossed on his phone. But only initially. One painful blink and he swam to the surface of her vision, the registering of exactly who he was such a shock to her system that she blinked again.

He was still there.

Her heart made the most enormous thump. Thanasis Antoniadis was sitting by her bedside.

Too confused to be frightened, she lifted her head. Well, tried. Another shooting pain stopped her lifting it more than a couple of inches.

Pale green eyes with lashes as dark as the pupils and rings encircling the irises suddenly locked onto hers.

She swallowed, a reflex that had nothing to do with the dryness of her throat. 'Where am I?' Whatever bed she was in, it wasn't her bed, and this was no room she'd been in before.

'Hospital.'

Her next blink was slightly less painful and she became aware that she had things stuck to her chest and that something had been injected into her hand…a medical drip?

'You were in a car accident.'

So that was what his voice sounded like. Honeyed coffee. A thought that struck her confused mind as absurd even as her hazy, confused mind wondered why she was fixating on Thanasis's voice rather than asking what the hell she was doing in hospital with her family's greatest enemy at her bedside. Or, rather, her stepfamily's greatest enemy.

Lucie had been only three years old when her mother left her father for the Greek shipping tycoon Georgios Tsaliki, and so her childhood and adolescence had been split between her father and his new family, and her mother, Georgios and his varying offspring. Varying because Lucie's mother was wife number four. To everyone's surprise, over two decades later, the marriage was still going strong. Lucie suspected this was because her mother maintained an extremely well-developed blind eye to Georgios's many infidelities, infidelities she must have factored in when marrying him seeing as she was wife number three's replacement.

As a result, Lucie had grown up in two wildly differing households. Stability and order had come from her real father. Chaos and fun had come from her stepfather, whose gregarious nature had him on excellent terms with all his ex-wives and the nine children they'd collectively popped out for him. Life for Georgios and his extended family had been one great big holiday, right until the money had run out earlier that year and his eldest son, Alexis, wrested control of the company.

Because the converse to Georgios's generous heart was also true—when he took against someone, they remained his enemy for life, and Georgios Tsaliki had no greater enemy than rival shipping tycoon Petros Antoniadis, and it was this mutual enmity to blame for the near destruction of both families' fortunes.

The original cause of the enmity between the two men was something Lucie knew only the bare bones of; a business partnership between two great friends turned sour. If there were more details than that she suspected both men had forgotten them, and now their mutual loathing and feud was simply one of those things, like the fact she barely touched five foot in height and had unmanageable black curls. One of those things like the fact Thanasis Antoniadis smelt as flipping wonderful as he looked.

She'd seen him in the flesh only once before. She'd been eighteen at the time and enjoying her last long Greek summer holiday. Athena, Lucie's sometime favourite Tsaliki offspring—Athena blew hot and cold—had invited her along to what she'd promised would be the party of the decade. They'd barely stepped into the apartment when Lucie had spotted the best-looking man in the entire world pouring himself a drink at the bar and had actually felt her jaw drop. There had been something familiar about him, which had made her think he must be a famous actor or model or something. Whatever he did for a living, he was the most gorgeous man she'd ever laid eyes on and she'd been unable to tear her gaze away, until Athena had grabbed her hand and in a high-pitched voice whispered, 'What's *he* doing here?'

Lucie had stared at her blankly.

'Thanasis Antoniadis,' she'd explained, panicking. 'If I'd known he was going to be here, I would never have come. Papa will *kill* me if he hears about this.'

Lucie had looked again at the man causing the usually unflappable Athena to have a semi-meltdown at the exact moment Thanasis had looked across the busy room... and fixed his gaze right on *her*. The frisson she'd felt snake up her spine was like nothing she'd experienced before, or since for that matter. She might very well still be there gawping at him if Athena hadn't dragged her away, hissing, 'Stop looking at him like that! We need to get out of here.'

And that had been that. Less than two minutes under a roof with him.

He'd been familiar because he was the spitting image of his father. Georgios regularly refreshed the photo of Petros Antoniadis he kept on his dartboard.

The man who'd captured her attention so vividly six years ago was now scrutinising her with a strained intensity she felt like a touch to her skin.

'How are you feeling?' he asked.

'My head hurts and I feel sick,' she croaked, scrutinising him in turn with an increasing wariness as the drilling in her head settled enough for her brain to start vaguely functioning properly. There was something about the room that made her think she must be in Greece, but that was impossible. She'd gone to sleep in her shared north London flat...hadn't she?

She couldn't remember going to bed.

He grimaced. 'That is to be expected. You took quite the knock.'

'What happened to me? What's going on? Why are you here?'

His neck extended, the nostrils of his long, pointed nose flaring. 'Your mouth sounds dry. Water?'

'Please. But tell me what's happened and why you're here.'

He poured water from a jug into a beaker and placed a straw in it, then stretched an arm to place the straw close to her mouth. 'You don't remember?'

She inched her face to the straw. Before taking a much-needed drink, she said, 'I know you're Thanasis Antoniadis but I don't know why I'm in hospital, seemingly in Greece, or why you of all people are with me.'

Something flickered in his eyes. 'Me of all people? And drink slowly or you will make yourself sick. Take sips.'

His heavily accented English was excellent, she thought absently as she savoured the crisp coolness of fresh water in her mouth and hoped it didn't react to the nausea swirling in her stomach. Lucie's Greek was fluent but nowhere near as good as Thanasis's English. 'Thank you.'

He gave a tight nod of acknowledgement and put the

beaker back on the table without his stare leaving her face. 'Me of all people?' he repeated.

'Why would you be here? Where's my family?' The more pertinent question, she dimly supposed, was why she wasn't terrified to have woken with the son of her stepfather's enemy by her bed; a brooding near-stranger who had to tower over her by well over a foot in height and probably weighed twice as much to boot. All that weight would be muscle, something she knew by the way his light blue shirt stretched across his chest. This man was in prime physical fitness. If he wanted, he could snap her bones with the ease of a cruel child snapping a bug's wings.

Instead of quailing at the thought, she had an absurd sense of certainty that Thanasis Antoniadis would never lay a hand on her, not in malice nor in anger. Absurd because she didn't know this man at all, only knew of him, and yet her certainty went hand in hand with the sense coming to life inside her that she *did* know him, as if they'd met before in a different life or a different world.

That must be some potent cocktail of drugs being pumped through her system, she thought. Her aching brain was being *wild*.

After a long pause, he said, 'Your mother is here and has gone to get something to eat, but tell me, why would I not be here?'

'Because we're strangers?' But there was uncertainty, the whisper of a memory floating in her aching head that could have been a dream. A busy restaurant. Alexis, Georgios and her mother.

There was another flickering in his eyes. 'What is the last thing you remember?'

'Getting back from work...' She blinked as the specific memory refused to form. 'No. Making myself a frittata.' She'd loaded it with feta—to Lucie's mind, there was no such thing as too much cheese—but try as she might, she couldn't conjure the memory of eating it, nor the mound of sweet potato fries she'd made to accompany it.

A sliver of fear snaked into her bloodstream. 'What date is it?'

The intensity of his stare increased, his full, sensuous lips tightening along with the skin around his fabulously high cheekbones. 'The twenty-eighth of July.'

She jolted in shock, the fear tightening its grip. How could it be the end of July?

'What date did you think it was?'

Lucie thought hard, remembered adding a meeting into her work planner. 'The twentieth of May.'

She blinked again. She hadn't eaten the frittata because her mother had called. She'd been in London and wanted to take Lucie out to dinner to discuss something...

The busy restaurant floated in her vision again. Her mother. Georgios. Alexis.

'They want me to marry you,' she blurted out, the words forming a beat before the memory. She met Thanasis's stare again. 'My family want me to marry you to save Tsaliki Shipping.'

His green eyes didn't blink. 'What else? What else do you remember?'

She shook her head in fear and frustration. 'Nothing. There's nothing else.'

The next pause stretched for an age. When he finally spoke, Thanasis's voice had lost the taut edge she'd only been barely aware it contained. 'Lucie, look at your wedding finger.'

Her heart seemed to go into stasis as she unclenched her hand and carefully lifted it, mindful of the medical line running through it. And then every atom in her body contracted with shock to see the sparkling diamond ring on it.

'This isn't possible,' Lucie whispered.

'You agreed to marry me,' he said quietly. 'Our wedding is in nine days.'

She could only gape at him.

'In nine days our two families will come together to celebrate the marital union of an Antoniadis and a Tsaliki, and the war that has caused so much destruction to both our families and businesses will be officially over.'

All she could think to say to this was, 'But Athena's a Tsaliki, not me. I'm a Burton.'

'To the world at large, Georgios considers you his own. You're a Tsaliki daughter and sister in all but blood and name.'

Wasn't that along the lines of what Alexis had said during the meal when he'd thrown the bombshell that, to save Tsaliki Shipping, the family needed her to marry Thanasis? She had only had vague snippets of memory of that evening and everything that followed was a complete blank, but she remembered enough to feel what she'd felt then—a bloom in her heart to be considered a real Tsaliki.

A tight-knit group despite being born from varying wives, the Tsaliki siblings had always welcomed Lucie into the gang during the long school holidays she'd spent with them, and always made sure to include her in everything, but she'd always had the underlying sense they never truly saw her as one of them, a feeling that extended to her half-brother Loukas, the only child her mother had borne Georgios. She'd always had the same underlying sense at her father's home too, a cuckoo in the nest who never fitted in, especially once her half-sisters were born.

Of all Lucie's half-siblings and stepsiblings, the only one she'd felt a real sense of kinship with had been Athena, Georgios's only daughter and the Tsaliki closest to Lucie in age, and even that sense of kinship had been dependent on Athena's varying moods. If Athena was to swish into the hospital room now, she would come armed either with flowers and chocolate or with a syringe to needle at Lucie with. She often reminded Lucie of a cat imperviously swiping its claws at some unfortunate rodent for no other reason than that it was bored.

Smothering a yawn, Lucie gazed again into Thanasis's eyes, wishing she could find in them the answers for everything her injured brain was refusing to reveal.

She had to fight her closing throat to say, 'Are you telling the truth? Did I really agree to marry you?'

He didn't blink. 'I do not lie.'

'As any good liar would say,' she pointed out. Thanasis was an Antoniadis, and, if Georgios was to be believed, all Antoniadises were born with forked tongues.

There was the slightest loosening of his full lips but
before he could respond, the door opened and a nurse
entered the room. When she saw Lucie's eyes were open,
she shot an accusatory glare at Thanasis, which she then
quickly tried to cover by making effusive noises about
Lucie being awake.

While the nurse checked the machine the things stuck
to Lucie's chest were attached to, Thanasis got smoothly
to his feet, his phone gripped in his large hand. 'I will
let your mother know you're awake.'

Utterly dazed, not entirely convinced she wasn't
dreaming, Lucie watched the man who'd once haunted
her dreams leave the room.

'She's awake,' Thanasis said curtly.

The reply was reverential. 'Thank God for that.'

'She remembers nothing.'

A silence that went on too long and then a slow, 'Nothing?'

'Her memories of the last two months appear to have
been wiped out.'

More silence. 'Have you filled her in?'

'She knows only that she agreed to the marriage.'

'Nothing else?'

'Nothing else,' he confirmed.

Another long, long silence. 'Then let us hope her memories stay wiped until after the wedding.'

Lucie's mother ended the call.

'He must be very much in love with you,' the nurse confided as she shone a torchlight into Lucie's eyes. 'It is the first time he has voluntarily left your side.'

Of all the revelations that had been thrown at her in the short time she'd been awake, that one came as the biggest shock.

Thanasis Antoniadis was *in love* with her?

'Do you think?' she asked doubtfully. Nothing in his body language had made that kind of impression on her, although, with the fuzziness of her mind and the gaping void in it, she couldn't really be sure about anything. If anything, she'd had a vague impression of being scrutinised with a watchful wariness, as if she were some kind of unpredictable wild animal with Thanasis tasked as her handler.

The nurse turned the medical torch off and slipped it into her top pocket. 'You have been here two days.'

This was certainly the day for shocks and revelations.

'Seriously?' That long?

'We had to keep you sedated.' A misty look came in the nurse's eyes. 'He has kept watch over you.'

Wow. He'd been sitting in that hard armchair the whole time?

And then Lucie remembered Thanasis had told her she'd been in a car accident. Funny how she'd been too engrossed in listening to his voice to bother listening to his words. And then she'd been too engrossed in discovering she was supposed to be marrying him to worry about the fact she was lying in a hospital bed feeling as sick as a parrot and with a seeming head injury.

'Am I very badly hurt?'

The nurse gently squeezed her hand. 'There are concerns but all your vital signs are looking good. I have paged the doctor—it is for her to explain what has happened to you.'

'My head?' she guessed, a guess greatly aided by Thanasis's earlier observation that her head hurting *was to be expected*. And also aided by her memories being wiped. She wondered if it accounted for the dreamlike state she was in or if that was the result of whatever drugs were being fed into her.

But maybe this wasn't just a dreamlike state but an actual dream, she wondered again, and as she thought this, Thanasis came back into the room, all tall, dark and brooding, accompanied by a woman whose demeanour immediately identified her as a doctor, and Lucie's mother.

One whiff of her mother's overpowering perfume was all the proof Lucie needed to know that this was no dream.

Lucie had to wait until Thanasis left the room to make some business calls before she could speak to her mother privately. She was exhausted, her stomach still unsettled, and all she really wanted to do was sleep, but this was too important to wait.

'Is it true?' she asked. 'Did I really agree to marry him?'

Her mother's perfectly painted lips smiled. 'Yes, my darling, you did, and I cannot begin to tell you how proud and grateful we all are for the sacrifices you're making for us.'

But Lucie's head was too fuzzy to think about sacrifices, even when her mother airily mentioned Lucie resigning her job so she could move to Greece. The few short hours she'd been awake had been like waking in some kind of twilight zone where up was down and left was right. She had a diamond ring on her finger given to her by a man who when she'd last fallen asleep had been her stepfamily's enemy. And, she supposed, by extension, *her* enemy.

'Mum...how do Thanasis and I get on? The nurse seems to think...' But it was too incomprehensible to vocalise.

'Seems to think what?' her mother prompted.

She had to drop her voice to a whisper to actually say it. 'She thinks he's in love with me.'

The black eyes Lucie had inherited flickered. There was a long hesitation before her mother said, 'It has been obvious to us all that strong emotions have developed between you.'

'So he does love me?'

A shorter hesitation. 'I am certain of it.'

'And am I in love with him?'

This time there was no hesitation at all. 'Yes, my darling, I do believe you are.'

Thanasis strode to the end of the corridor by the fire exit, checked no one was within earshot, and made the call.

Alexis answered on the second ring. 'Is it true?'

'Yes. She has amnesia.'

'How long until her memories come back?'

'Unknown. Could be days. Could be months. They might never come back.'

'Who knows what happened between the two of you?'

'You, your father and Lucie's mother.'

'Not your parents?'

'Obviously they know about the accident but not what went on before. Have you told anyone else?'

'No.'

Thanasis thought hard and quickly. If it was only the four of them who knew the full truth, they could keep it contained. 'What about Athena?'

'She knows nothing.'

'Keep it that way. And keep her away from the hospital. She's a loose cannon.'

He heard Alexis suck in a breath at the slight to his only sister, but Thanasis didn't care. Of all the Tsalikis, Athena had proven herself to have the most poisonous sting. 'The press have been tipped off about the accident,' he said. 'The hospital's security team have moved them off the grounds but they are waiting to ambush her as soon as she's discharged.'

It went without saying that Lucie abhorred the press, and it was a mark of her affection and loyalty to the monster that was Georgios Tsaliki that she'd willingly put herself in the media's spotlight to save his fortune.

'When will that be?' Alexis asked.

'A couple of days at least. When she's released, I will take her to my island—no one can reach her there. In the meantime, I propose we put out a short statement confirming the accident and confirm that she is recovering well and that the wedding is going ahead as planned.'

'Is it?'

Thanasis closed his eyes, recalling the message Lucie's mother had sent him only a few minutes earlier.

She believes you were in love. Unless you want her to run again, play along with it until the wedding.

'If her memories stay lost and your sister keeps her mouth shut then yes, I am certain Lucie will honour the agreement.'

'Good.'

A figure stepped into the corridor. Rebecca Tsaliki. Lucie's mother.

Thanasis met her stare and felt a wave of loathing towards the Englishwoman. Bad enough that he and Alexis were planning to use Lucie's amnesia to their advantage, but this was her mother conspiring against her.

'I need to go,' he said curtly into the phone.

'Keep me updated.'

'Likewise.'

'And, Thanasis?'

'Yes?'

'I suggest you play things differently with her this time. For all our sakes.'

# CHAPTER TWO

THANASIS ENDED THE CALL, rolled his tense neck and slowly filled his lungs with air.

Barely two days ago he'd thought his world on the brink of collapse.

'You're an immoral, lying bastard and I'd rather marry a plague-ridden rat than marry you!' Lucie had screamed before snatching the keys to his Porsche 911 from his hands.

'I never lied to you,' he'd retorted furiously. 'Now give them back.'

She'd delivered a curse of such uncouth viciousness that he'd recoiled. Never in his life had he been on the receiving end of such an insult, not even from Lucie.

If he hadn't recoiled, none of what followed would have happened. If he'd kept his wits he'd have been able to take his keys from her without any force—Lucie was easily half his size and weight—and she wouldn't have had time to storm out of his penthouse shouting, 'The wedding is *off* and I don't care what the world thinks. I never want to see you again. I hope you have a *horrible* life.'

He'd chased after her. Of course he had. Lucie had been like a human grenade whose pin had been released, and there had been no telling how far her explosion would spread. He'd stepped into his foyer as the elevator doors had closed and so had raced down the seven flights of stairs and reached the underground car park to find her reversing out of his space with the clunking of gears and the screeching of wheels, whereupon she'd spun the car towards the exit and put her foot down, flipping him the bird as she'd passed for good measure. He had no doubt that if he'd stood in front of the car in the hope of stopping her, she'd have hit the accelerator even harder.

She couldn't call the marriage off, he'd tried to assure himself even as he'd made the terse call to Alexis to inform him of what had happened. If the Antoniadises went down then so did the Tsalikis. Everyone would lose.

The decades-long feud between the patriarchs had escalated as they'd aged to the extent that the dirty tricks they'd employed had escalated too, dangerously so, dirty tricks the press had got wind of. What had been an infamous rivalry enjoyed by the public swirled into a maelstrom of relentless negative publicity that had led to investors threatening to pull out of Antoniadis Shipping. Thanasis's father had voluntarily stepped down his position as Chief Executive, the board of directors voting unanimously for Thanasis to step into his shoes, but this hadn't been enough to mollify the investors.

At the precise moment Thanasis had been wondering how the hell he was going to stop his company imploding, Alexis Tsaliki, who'd not long forced his own father from the board of Tsaliki Shipping, had called requesting a private meeting. 'Our fathers' actions caused all this,' he'd said. 'It is for us to end it.'

What had followed had started out like a scene from a gangster film where the new heads of two families fighting over the same territory had faced off.

The deadlock had been broken when Alexis had said, 'The only way to stem the losses we are both suffering is to show we are serious about ending our fathers' feud. I propose a marriage.'

'An intriguing idea but you're not my type,' Thanasis had deadpanned, even as he'd immediately seen the sick logic behind the suggestion.

'A shame. We would make a beautiful couple. But no, I propose a marriage between myself and your sister.'

'Over my dead body,' he'd stated flatly. Alexis Tsaliki was poison like all Tsalikis, and an unscrupulous Lothario. Thanasis would sooner live bankrupt in a shed than countenance a marriage with his sister to him.

They'd eyeballed each other for a time that had seemed to suck all the air from the room, until Alexis had given a sharp nod. 'Then you will have to be the one to make the sacrifice.'

And that was how, eventually, Thanasis had come to be engaged to Lucie Burton, Georgios's so-called beloved stepdaughter and the so-called beloved daughter of Rebecca Tsaliki.

Rebecca stepped over to him. Voice low, she said, 'You got my message?'

He nodded curtly.

'Then you know what to do.'

He didn't bother hiding his disdain. Now he understood how this wife had succeeded where Georgios's other wives had failed—her ruthlessness. That this extended to her own daughter sickened him, even if he did despise the daughter as much as the mother.

'How could you let her believe we'd fallen in love?' he demanded.

'I didn't put the idea in her head, I just ran with it,' she answered, her own disdain as evident as his. 'What did you expect me to say? That she was mistaken and you hate each other's guts?'

'No, I would have expected you to correct her and tell her our relationship was cordial and businesslike.'

'If you'd kept it cordial and businesslike we wouldn't be standing here.'

That this observation was on the money only added to the burning angst pumping through him.

'You need to be nice to her for a week,' Rebecca said in the same acidic tone he'd heard her daughter use more times than were countable. 'That's it. Be nice, and get her to the damned church to make her vows. After that, you can do whatever you want with her.'

They both knew Lucie would never sell them out to the press. Even when she'd furiously screeched away in his Porsche, Thanasis had been certain her intense aversion to being public property would stop her taking that nuclear step. Whether she took that step or not though was irrelevant—her failure to marry him would set off a nuclear detonation of its own.

'I will go along with this pathetic charade until the wedding because you leave me no other choice, but you'd better pray her memories don't come back before it.'

'We should all pray for that.'

He shook his head in disbelief. 'When she learns the truth… She will hate you for facilitating the lies. You know that, yes? You could lose your daughter for this.'

Rebecca was unmoved. 'If that's the price I have to pay then I can live with that. All that matters is that the wedding goes ahead. Anything that comes after can and will be managed. We'll pay her off if necessary—she pretended not to care but I know she was jealous of Georgios's brood having their own trust funds. Cold hard cash always makes injured feelings sting a little less.'

Sickened to his core, Thanasis turned without another word and strode with heavy footsteps back to Lucie's room.

Before entering, he took a moment to compose himself.

The path had been set and he had to follow it. The alternative would be devastation for everyone and everything.

Their engagement had stemmed much of the press negativity and calmed the investors, but there had been predicted cynicism too. If the wedding failed to go ahead the media would go into a frenzy, the becalmed investors likely pull their investments.

In only three weeks, Antoniadis Shipping would take

delivery of fifty new container ships to add to their fleet at a cost of close to six billion euros. Two thirds of this still needed to be paid. If the investors pulled out, Thanasis would have to conjure four billion euros. Antoniadis Shipping was worth tens of billions but that money wasn't sitting in a bank account. It would take months to liquidate enough assets to cover it.

All these things had been going through his head as he'd tried to work out how the hell he was going to steer his company away from the impending disaster when he'd received the call that Lucie had been in an accident.

Thanasis's luck had turned one-eighty, but this luck was on a knife-edge. Lucie's amnesia was a blessing but he couldn't predict how long it would last, and now he was being forced into a risky game that upped the stakes considerably.

It was time to up the game to match the stakes and step into the shoes of the man Lucie thought him to be. If her memories returned before the wedding she'd run from his life all over again, and this time she really would destroy everything.

By the time night fell on Lucie's third day in hospital—technically her fifth but she didn't count the first two as she'd been sedated—she was seriously contemplating asking the medical team to sedate her mother. If she'd known it would take a traumatic head injury to make her do some actual mothering, she'd never have got behind a wheel because her mother's definition of actual mothering was doing Lucie's poorly head in. It was the non-stop chatter about the wedding, the constant emphasis about how wonderful it was all going to be, what a beautiful couple Lucie and Thanasis made and what a happy marriage they were going to have, how wonderful it was that the feud between the two families had come to an end because of it, plus the constant need to fill Lucie in on all the details about the wedding itself, the world-famous singers who'd be performing for them, the guest list, the catering, yada-yada-yada. All this while constantly watching Lucie with an anxious scrutiny she'd not shown a shred of when Lucie had caught the flu over the Christmas holidays a decade ago. The only Tsaliki to brave a visit had been Athena, who quite rightly assumed no germ would dare latch itself into her system. When Lucie had finally recovered from it, she'd been surprised to find her mother hadn't marked her bedroom door with a big red X.

All her mum's chattering meant she'd found herself grateful for all the sleep her body currently demanded. Lots and lots of sleep. So much sleep that she could feel herself coming out of the fog, becoming more lucid and less dreamlike. She didn't feel sick any more either, which was a blessing because Lucie hated feeling sick; hated feeling too ill to eat. Give her a headache over sickness any day of the week. And now she had neither, although she was certain her headache would be back with a vengeance at the rate her mother was talking. If she didn't know better, she'd assume her mother was deliberately distracting her from having to think.

For all that her mother was doing her head in, in

one respect she was grateful for this late onset maternal blossoming—her mother's constant presence meant she'd only spent snatches of time alone with Thanasis.

Like her mother, he was a constant presence at Lucie's bedside. Unlike her mother, he rarely spoke, which in fairness was because her mum never stopped talking long enough for him to get a word in edgeways.

He rarely spoke but every time Lucie glanced at him she found his green gaze on her. Every time, a frisson would snake up her spine.

With no memories to fall back on it was impossible to know if she really had fallen in love with this man but her reactions were telling her she'd felt *something* for him. And, as incredible as it was to believe, something in the way he looked at her told her he'd felt something for her too, and she didn't know if it was relief or anxiety she felt when her mother finally announced she was going home to get some sleep. The other times her mother had left her alone with Thanasis, Lucie had been deep in sleep herself.

'I'll be back in the morning in time for the results of your scan, darling,' she said as she placed a kiss to Lucie's forehead. 'Let's hope they give you the all-clear to be discharged.'

Lucie smiled wanly. 'Fingers crossed.'

She watched her mother swish to the door, certain she wasn't imagining the significant look she threw at Thanasis before she disappeared through it. Lucie would have wondered what the look was about if she hadn't been so immediately aware that she was alone with the stranger she was shortly to marry.

A stranger she instinctively knew without her mother having to keep banging on about it that she shared something with, a short but significant history her brain refused to reveal.

It took an immense amount of courage to turn her face to him.

Their eyes locked.

'Is it just me or have you suddenly gone deaf too?' she asked, going into her default mode of cracking a joke to cover an awkward silence even though it wasn't awkward she was predominantly feeling but, inexplicably, shy. Lucie couldn't remember ever feeling shy, not once in her whole life.

Lines appeared around his eyes as his perfect teeth flashed before his expression softened and he hunched forward to gently cover her hand. 'How are you really feeling, *matia mou*?'

'Better. Much less fuzzy.' Although the sensation of Thanasis's hand on hers made her glad the medical team had detached the sticky things on her chest that measured her heart rate, or the whole hospital staff would be kicking the door down to see what had caused the massive spike in it.

He was just so dreamily handsome, with his dark brown hair and thick stubble, and the deep olive hue of his skin and those mesmerising eyes and full lips. As hard as she looked, she couldn't find a single flaw, not unless you counted the lines that formed around his eyes when he gave one of his rare smiles, which she didn't because they gave perfection an extra dimension.

'That is good to hear.' Broad shoulders lifting, he rubbed his thumb over her palm sending sensation dancing through her skin. 'Do you feel well enough in yourself to go home if the scans show it's safe?'

She nodded, then hesitated before asking, 'Where is home for me now?'

'With me.' He bowed his head and gently brushed his lips to her fingers.

Warm breath danced fleetingly over her skin. The beats of her heart spiked again.

So it *was* true. They had fallen for each other, and as this thought swirled, she thought of the Montagues and Capulets…and then remembered how that particular story ended and quickly strove for a different comparison.

'Do we live in Athens?' she asked when no other comparison came to her.

'We have been, but when you are discharged I would like to take you to Sephone.' At her uncomprehending look, he smiled. It was like being doused in a ray of sunlight. 'Sephone is my island.'

'You have your own island? Seriously?'

'When we are married it will be *our* island. It is a secluded paradise. You will love it there, I promise.'

'You've not taken me before?'

'There hasn't been the time, but as you need peace to recover and we are due to marry there, it is the perfect setting for you to recuperate before our big day…that is if you still want to marry me?' He posed the question casually but there was a shadowy flickering in his eyes that made her pulses thump.

He was frightened her amnesia would make her change her mind, she realised.

'I know your mother has done her best to impress on you how far advanced our wedding preparations are, but I will understand if you want to postpone it and give your memories the chance to come back,' he said quietly, her hand now swallowed whole inside both of his. 'If you'd rather call the whole thing off…obviously it would make things difficult from a business perspective but that is the least of my concerns. You and your health are my primary concerns, so if you want to postpone or cancel altogether, do not be afraid to say. I only want what is best for you.'

A dizzying rush of blood filled Lucie's head.

He really did have feelings for her. Feelings enough to take the pressure of the wedding off her shoulders and give her brain the chance to heal even though the consequences for his business would likely be disastrous.

Close to being overwhelmed with the emotions being evoked by this man who was a stranger and yet with whom… Her heart skipped as her thoughts jumped.

If she already lived with this man then she was already sharing his bed…

Heat to power a small house suffused her from the inside out.

She'd shared a bed with Thanasis. Made love to him.

Concern creased his forehead. 'You are flush, *matia mou*. Are you in pain?'

But that only deepened the heat scorching her, and she gave a quick, frantic shake of her head. No way was she going to confess what was going on in her head, not to a stranger, especially not a male one. The embarrassment would kill her. Whatever intimacies they'd shared, she had no memories of them.

'You are sure?' he pressed.

She drew in a long breath as she practically pinned her thoughts into submission so she could think and speak coherently. 'Thanasis, I have no recollection of anything about our engagement or wedding plans but I know in my heart that I did promise to marry you. I've never broken a promise before and I'm not going to start now.'

The corners of his mouth twitched. 'I would understand if you wanted time to start over. You must feel at a great disadvantage.'

'It's frustrating more than anything,' she confessed. 'It must be frustrating for you too. You and I have a history together but my stupid brain is taking us back to step one in the getting-to-know-you stakes.'

He turned her hand and pressed his mouth to her palm. 'I would rather be on the first step with you than no step.'

The whole of her body sighed, and as his face inched closer to hers and the connection of the lock of their eyes deepened, anticipation pulsed into life and she held her breath...

He gently released her hand and gave a rueful twist

of his lips. 'It is getting late,' he said, inching his chair back. 'I will leave you to sleep.'

If there was one thing Thanasis had learned in the two months he'd spent getting to know Lucie Burton, it was that she was incapable of hiding her emotions, and he felt a flare of satisfaction mingled with guilt to see disappointment flash over her face.

'I will be back before you wake, but I haven't been home in five days.' He shook off the guilt. If Lucie had taken one damn minute to hear him out, none of this would have happened, but the pin on the grenade of her temper had spent weeks a hair trigger away from being pulled out. If it hadn't been Athena it would have been something or someone else. Lucie's mother had forced him into playing the role of loving fiancé but Lucie's actions had caused the necessity for it. 'You need to sleep and I need to make arrangements to get you safely to Sephone and ensure all your medical needs can be taken care of.'

'There's nothing wrong with my body, only my head.'

There was *everything* wrong with her body, and it took every ounce of self-control not to let his attentive fiancé mask drop and his revulsion show.

The revulsion was entirely for himself.

Thanasis had prepared himself to loathe Lucie. He could forgive Georgios's blood children for loving their father and being loyal to him but Lucie chose to love him. She'd voluntarily chosen to sacrifice her life in England to save his fortune. She'd freely given her love and loyalty to a monster, which to Thanasis's mind meant she condoned the monster and so made her equally despicable.

His first meeting with her had been after the terms of the marriage had been negotiated and agreed between himself and Alexis. A marriage in name only, one that would last a few years before they quietly went their separate ways. Their fathers had been given no choice but to fall in line with their plan. With everything agreed, the only thing left to do...apart from arrange the wedding... was for Thanasis to meet his 'bride'.

The meet had taken place in the neutral territory of an exclusive hotel's bar. Alexis had made the call and minutes later a tiny waif with a mop of long black curls had appeared. Just one look had been enough for Thanasis's heart to explode.

Dear God in heaven, it was *her*.

His mind had flown back six years to Leander's party and the waif dressed all in black and with black hair piled on top of her head like a curly pineapple. A tiny, tiny creature with the most strikingly beautiful face he'd ever set eyes on.

It had been the only time in his life he'd experienced that 'eyes meeting across the room moment'. Before he'd had the chance to cross the floor to her and introduce himself, her friend, a blur to his eyes like every other face in the apartment had been in that moment, had dragged her away, not just from the room they'd entered but from the apartment itself. She'd vanished.

He'd asked Leander about her but Leander hadn't

known who he was talking about. Neither had anyone else.

For months he'd been unable to drive or walk a street in Athens without casting an eye for a diminutive waif with black curly hair, but he'd never seen her again. In time, he'd convinced himself that he'd imagined her.

But she'd been real.

She'd strolled—although *bounced* would be a more accurate description—into the hotel bar wearing a loose-fitting, sleeveless black dress patterned with blood-red roses that fell to her knees. On her feet had been a pair of calf-length clumpy black boots. Her hair had been worn loose, cascades of curls springing in all directions. She'd looked like a cross between a modern-day Bride of Frankenstein and an ethereally beautiful elf. Except elves were supposed to have big, pointy ears and he'd been unable to see anything of her ears through the mass of curls.

Lucie, a beam on her face and expectation shining in eyes as black as her hair, had stepped to Thanasis with arms outstretched as if expecting an embrace.

Up close, her beauty had shone as much as the shine in her black eyes, and there had been a beat when he'd been powerless to do anything but soak in the oversized eyes and pretty little nose and full heart-shaped lips, all set on a flawless golden heart-shaped canvas.

His heart thumping hard enough to rattle his ribs, he'd pointedly held his hand out.

It was her hesitation before slipping her tiny hand into his that had confirmed in his mind that she too remembered that brief moment of connection from six years earlier, but it was the jolt of electricity that had powered through him at the connection of their skin that had made his jaw clench.

'Nice boots,' he'd said acidly, pulling his hand from her clasp.

The shine in her eyes had dimmed into confusion before her little heart-shaped chin had defiantly lifted. 'It's lovely to meet you too.'

If not hugely aware that time had been ticking to save his company, Thanasis would have called a halt to the agreement there and then.

He'd been fully prepared to marry someone he despised, prepared to spend a few years swallowing his loathing for the good of everything that mattered in his world: his mother, who'd always shaken her head at her husband's rivalry with Georgios Tsaliki, his father, who for all his faults had been a loving father and husband, his sister, who'd become increasingly gaunt and withdrawn since the extent of the rivalry between Antoniadis and Tsaliki had been made public, and the thousands and thousands of people Antoniadis Shipping employed.

What he'd not been prepared for was attraction. Not to someone who'd spent her life in the Tsaliki nest and who considered Georgios Tsaliki a father figure.

Attraction was the last thing he'd expected or wanted, and that he should feel it so powerfully for the captivatingly beautiful Lucie Burton had been additional nails in the coffin of his loathing for her.

By the time she'd screeched away in his Porsche, she'd hated him as much as he hated her, and now he had to remind himself of the expectant shine in her eyes when she'd bounced into that hotel bar all those long weeks ago. There had been hope in that shine too, a hope he'd scotched with his first words to her.

Lucie's amnesia had granted him a reset, a means to play things differently, and he had no intention of screwing it up again.

Speaking steadily, he captured a curl in a manner that could only be interpreted as affectionate. 'Every part of you is too precious for me to risk your health.'

She gave a sigh as soft as the curl in his fingers. 'I'll do everything I can to get the memories back.'

Exactly what he didn't want to hear.

'Just concentrate on healing, *matia mou*, and let the memories take care of themselves.' And then, because he knew he must, he bowed his head, held his breath, and pressed a kiss so chaste to Lucie's mouth he barely felt the pressure of it.

It wasn't chaste enough to stop his heart pumping harder and faster, and it took even more control not to recoil into retreat.

With unhurried movements, he got to his feet, but his escape was thwarted when she caught his hand.

Black eyes gazing up at him with a solemnity he'd never seen in them before, she quietly said, 'I was raised to despise your family. It was instilled in all of us that the Antoniadises were spawns of the devil. The loyalty and affection I feel towards Georgios means I would have agreed to marry you even if I had believed the indoctrination. I would have married the devil himself if it had meant saving Tsaliki Shipping. But I never did believe it, not really, and now you've proved I was right not to.' There was an almost imperceptible catch in her husky voice. 'Thank you for being here for me.'

Thanasis's throat had closed so tightly it was an effort to speak. *'Parakalo,'* he whispered hoarsely.

He left the room with his lips still abuzz from the barely-there pressure of Lucie's mouth, and with the skin of his hand burning as if her touch had marked it.

# CHAPTER THREE

BACK HOME IN his Athens apartment, Thanasis set everything in motion so all Lucie's medical needs would be taken care of upon her discharge. That done, he checked in with the chief wedding planner, uncaring that the sleepiness in Griselda's voice meant he'd woken her. The extortionate price he was paying for her services meant she was on call twenty-four-seven.

The call finished with reassurances that Lucie was recovering well, and then Thanasis headed up to his room for a shower, passing Lucie's room as he went. He'd get a member of the staff to pack her belongings. He would need them to pack a smaller case with clothes for her to choose from for when she was discharged too. It was inconceivable that he'd bring Lucie back here to supervise the packing of her possessions. If anything was going to trigger her memories, it would be this apartment, home to virtually every bitter exchange between them.

As per the detailed plan drawn up between himself and Alexis, she'd moved in a couple of weeks after the announcement of their engagement.

He'd installed her in the guest room furthest from

his own but it hadn't been far enough. The few public appearances they'd made together up to that point had been hell. Holding her hand without flinching and forcing his features into something that resembled that of a loving fiancé had taken acting skills he hadn't known he possessed.

It had been Lucie who, off the cuff, had murmured to a cynical journalist that they'd fallen for each other during peace talks between the two families. A stroke of genius he hadn't wanted to admire her for. He didn't want to admire anything about her.

He could not bear to be enclosed in the same walls as her.

Being affectionate in public had taken acting skills on Lucie's part too. In public, she'd played her part perfectly, all doe eyes and soft smiles even though having the paparazzi's cameras aimed at her face was a form of torture for her. The moment they were alone, her black eyes would flash their loathing and her nose wrinkle its disdain. He'd lost count of the times she'd wiped her freed hand on her clothes as if wiping the feel of him off her skin, her back stiff and turned from him. Lost count of the times he'd done the same.

It had never worked, and that was what had made everything so much harder to endure. Every time their hands clasped, he felt the burn of her skin against his for hours after. Every time he slipped an arm around her waist as a show of affection for the cameras and she leaned into him for the same reason, he'd find himself breathing in the scent of her hair and find himself still inhaling it when alone in his bed. Still feeling the soft tickle of it against his neck. Still feeling the compression of her slight figure against his torso. Still feeling his heated blood coursing through his veins.

If they'd met under different circumstances, as genuine strangers with no entwined family histories and no bad blood, then things would be a whole lot different. He would bed her in a heartbeat and get this all-consuming ache for her out of his system.

It was the age-old conundrum of forbidden fruit, he acknowledged grimly as he stripped off his clothes. Being forbidden always made an object infinitely more tempting. As a child he'd been forbidden from using the swimming pool without adult supervision. The first time unsupervised opportunity had presented itself, he'd dive-bombed into the pool. If not for the racket his dive-bomb had made, the gardener would never have thought to look and would never have seen four-year-old Thanasis struggling to keep his head above water.

Lucie was more off limits than the swimming pool had been.

To Thanasis's mind, marriage was the ultimate commitment two people could make, and sacred for it. When he made that commitment in the future, it would be for love and it would be for ever, and he would not allow any aspect of his temporary marriage to feel real enough to taint that future. When he made his real vows, he wanted to join his real wife in his real marital bed knowing it was the first time for him to make love as a husband.

His anger rising, he stepped under the shower.

Why the hell hadn't he demanded a photo of Lucie before agreeing to marry her? Thanks to varying European privacy laws concerning minors, there were no pictures of her in the public domain, and the private life she'd lived in England since turning eighteen meant she'd escaped the paparazzi's attention. If he'd known it was her, the woman who'd captivated him with that one look across a room all those years ago, he'd have played hard ball and demanded Athena or no deal. There would be no temptation of forbidden fruit there. Athena was beautiful too, but it was a beauty that left him cold.

And now he had to spend the next week walking a tightrope playing the devoted fiancé to a woman who made him feel anything but cold.

'Wouldn't it be better for me to spend a few days in Athens before we go to Sephone?' Lucie said the next morning after the medical team left the room. Her latest scan results had been discussed, the doctor declaring her well enough to be discharged. This had resulted in her mother immediately diving into the carry-on case Thanasis had brought from the apartment for this eventuality and Thanasis getting straight onto the phone. It seemed her mother and fiancé were working in cahoots to get her out of this hospital room as soon as humanly possible.

'Why would you think that, darling?' her mother asked, shaking out a black summer dress with a wrinkle of her nose.

'Maybe because the doctor just said one of the best ways to aid the recovery of my memories is by going to familiar places,' Lucie pointed out drily. 'I've never been to Sephone.'

'The doctor also said you need to rest, and what better place than a peaceful island unless you *want* the paparazzi to stalk you?'

Lucie shuddered at the mere thought. If anything had tainted her childhood, it had been the paparazzi's near constant presence during her time spent in Greece. Her mother's love of the intrusive spotlight was but one of the many fundamental differences between them.

Her mother handed the dress to her. 'Do you still not own clothes that aren't black?'

Lucie looked at the tightly fitting, high-fashion, colourful attire her mother was wearing and chose not to answer. She was long past the rebellious teenage years when she'd adopted dressing from head to toe in black as a silent means of needling the woman who'd given birth to her, but old habits died hard. She'd added splashes of colour to her wardrobe in recent years but still felt most comfortable wearing black.

'Excuse me a moment,' Thanasis murmured, shifting from his position at the window where he'd been deep in conversation. 'I need to make a call that might involve shouting.'

Startled at the glimpse of humour from a man she'd assumed didn't possess one—in all their time in this hospital room, he'd been nothing but serious—Lucie grinned.

She'd woken with a clearer head than she'd had since coming round from the sedation and spent a blissful hour in peace and solitude with nothing but her thoughts to occupy her. But, instead of searching for her lost memories, she'd spent the time wondering what it was about Thanasis that had made her fall for him. Apart from his devastating dark good looks and perfect body that was. She'd had the odd date with good-looking men over the years but always something had put her off wanting a second date. Usually it was too much vanity or a lack of humour, often both—she found those two traits went hand in hand—and so she'd pondered what it was Thanasis had the others lacked and how she could fall for so serious a man, and now she knew. He *did* have a tiny, latent sense of humour behind the Mr Serious persona.

'Is my phone in the case?' she asked her mother once they were alone. It was the first time she'd even thought of it. She dreaded to think how many messages she'd have to reply to.

Sighing at the inconvenience, her mother had a quick rummage in Lucie's case. 'Not that I can see. Do you need help dressing?'

'I could do with a shower first.' Since being admitted into hospital she'd had to put up with the nurses giving her bed baths, which would have been the indignity from hell if she hadn't been so spaced out on the drugs, but now she was actually *compos mentis* she'd rather pluck each individual leg hair out than put up with that again. She wanted a shower. A long, lovely shower.

'There isn't time,' her mother dismissed. 'Another patient will need this room.'

'But the nurse said there was no rush.'

'She was being polite. Come on, get that dreadful plastic gown off you.'

It took an incredible effort not to go into sulky teenager mode. 'Underwear?'

Once everything had been placed on the armchair for Lucie to change into, she gave her mother a meaningful look. 'Some privacy?'

Her mother rolled her eyes. 'You always were a prudish little thing.' Magicking a bulging makeup bag from nowhere, she disappeared into the adjoining bathroom with mutters of 'touching up her face'.

Lucie glared at the closed bathroom door. She'd always hated it when her mother teased her for being a prude. Just because she'd made it to twenty-four with only one real boyfriend under her belt, and preferred wearing loose-fitting clothes that covered her breasts and backside rather than the tight miniskirts and low crop tops her mother favoured, did not mean she was prudish.

She stepped into her knickers, her grumpiness melting away as Thanasis filled her mind again. Had he seen her in these knickers? Stripped them from her?

What had it been like between them? Disappointing like her past experience? Or had it been good? Even pleasurable?

Thanasis knew his way around a woman's body enough to make it pleasurable, she decided as she removed the dreadful—her mother had been right about that—hospital gown. You could just tell. Although she didn't know how she could just tell.

Letting the gown fall to the floor, she reached for her

bra, searching as hard as she could in the void of her brain for any memory of sleeping with him.

What had his touch felt like? Had she burned for him? Remembering how the touch of his hand had sent her heart rate spiking and how the gentle kiss he'd placed on her mouth the night before had turned her belly into mush, she thought she must have. Closing her eyes, she made a silent plea for those particular memories to come back. Even if all the other memories stayed lost for ever, please bring those ones back to her. Please, please.

'Lucie, we—'

Not having heard or even sensed the door opening, she whipped her head round and caught Thanasis frozen in mid-step at the door. Slamming her arms across her exposed breasts, she gripped her biceps, bra dangling from her fingers, embarrassment at being caught semi-naked scorching her in a white-hot flame.

A beat that seemed to last a lifetime passed between them, the dark pulse in his stare turning the flame of embarrassment into a different kind of burn, the kind of burn she'd been imagining only moments ago when wondering what it had felt like being made love to by him.

And then he blinked and the dark pulse vanished as he took a step back and a visible shutter came down in his eyes. 'I apologise—I should have knocked.'

Realising her reaction must make her seem like the prude her mum had just accused her of being, a fresh batch of mortification enflamed her skin, and she lifted her chin with a bravado she absolutely did not feel inside and went into default jocular mode. 'No, no, it's fine.

Not your fault. Of course you didn't need to knock. I'm your fiancée and it's not like you haven't seen my boobs before… It's just that I don't remember the before.'

His jaw tightened a fraction before he gave a brief nod and took hold of the door handle. 'Understood. I'll leave you to dress.'

He closed the door with the same stealthy silence he'd opened it.

Her heart now threatening to explode out of her ribs, Lucie sank onto her bed and tried to catch her breath.

Thanasis stood beneath the air conditioning unit and blew out a long puff of air. A sheen of perspiration had broken out over his skin.

Closing his eyes, he clenched his fists and refilled his lungs.

*Theos*, that body.

It was perfect. That was the only word to describe it. Perfect. Perfection enhanced by the plainness of her black underwear, which created such a strong contrast with the lightness of her golden skin. Perfect gentle curves. Small but perfectly shaped breasts he knew with one look would sit perfectly cupped in the palm of his hands.

He expelled another long, tortured breath and pressed his head against the wall, closing his eyes even tighter to drive the image of semi-naked Lucie from his vision.

*Theos*, from the heavy thrumming in his veins, you would think it was the first time he'd seen a pair of naked breasts in the flesh.

What made the rush of arousal pulsing through him more intolerable was the beat that had passed between them before he'd found his voice to apologise.

In that beat, the filter had slipped off them both and the unwanted, unacknowledged desire that had always simmered between them had been a shimmering, living entity.

A violent blush crawled over Lucie's face the second she heard the tap on the door. She had no idea how she was able to call out, 'Come in,' in a voice that sounded in any way normal, and when Thanasis stepped into the room, she felt the blush deepen and spread.

To her immense gratitude, he gave not a single sign that he'd walked in on her practically naked only minutes earlier, and she was beyond grateful that he accepted and understood so well that everything they'd shared together was lost to her.

'My driver is here,' he said in that glorious deep, honeyed tone. 'Are you ready to go?'

She nodded, still unable to meet his stare. 'Before we leave, have you seen my phone?'

He cast his gaze around the room. 'It isn't here?'

'Not that we've found. Was it recovered from the accident?' The accident she still only knew the barest details of, namely that she'd borrowed one of Thanasis's cars and crashed it. She'd been too fuzzy of head to think of asking more questions about it, but one thing she didn't need to question was that she would have had it on her. Lucie never went anywhere without her phone.

'All the personal possessions you had at the time of the accident were put in the cupboard by your bed.'

'I've looked there.'

'I will ask the garage where the car's being repaired and see if they have found it.'

'Can you do that now, please? I need to check in with my dad, and Kelly and…' There was a pang in her chest to know she was no longer an employee of Kelly Holden Designs. Lucie had loved her job as an interior designer. Really loved it. Her resignation was another void in her brain. So too giving up her share of the flat tenancy. 'Check in with my whole life really.'

Thanasis gave a brief, tight smile. 'Of course.'

With everything that had been going on, he hadn't given Lucie's phone a second thought, but now he knew it was missing, he could only hope it stayed lost.

Thanasis's family and the Tsalikis would all keep their mouths shut about the animosity between them but he had no way of knowing what she'd confided to others. He was confident she'd not betrayed the pact they'd made before their final argument but Lucie's fury when she'd left his apartment that day was such that it was within the realm of possibility she would have called one of her many friends to vent about it.

The call to the garage was over within a minute.

'I'm afraid your phone wasn't in the car,' he told her, relief filling him.

Fate, it seemed, was determined to continue working in his favour.

'I have your father's number,' he added. 'You can use

my phone to check in with him.' Thanasis had spoken to Charlie Burton numerous times since the accident and was confident Lucie had confided nothing in him.

'If we stop at a phone shop on our way to the harbour, I can buy myself a replacement,' she suggested.

He made a point of looking at his watch. 'It's a long sail to Sephone. The sooner we set off the better.' And the more isolated he kept her, the less likely something or someone would trigger her memories. 'I can have a phone helicoptered to you, if you wish.'

'Can't we take the helicopter ourselves?'

'No flying until you are back to full health,' he asserted firmly, and was rewarded with such a doe-eyed look that the guilt at his deception plunged a little deeper.

Damn Rebecca Tsaliki for letting her daughter believe they were lovers. And damn himself for going along with it.

Lying did not come naturally to Thanasis but what other choice did he have? Let his business be destroyed and his family face destitution?

And besides, if Lucie's memories came back before the wedding, they were all damned however they played it. The resulting explosion would lead to a scorched earth.

It was only for another week, he reminded himself grimly. Not even that. Six days. Just until they made their vows. The most pressing thing was getting her to the altar and the world's press witnessing Antoniadis and Tsaliki breaking bread together for the first time in forty years.

But as much as Thanasis needed to get Lucie swiftly away from Athens and to the solitude of his island, he would not disregard the doctor's advice. Flying the short distance—and by helicopter, it was a short distance—should be safe for her he'd been assured, but to his mind *should* was not cast-iron enough. His feelings for Lucie were a hot mess of lust and loathing but he would never wish physical harm on her or do anything to put her in danger.

He could still feel remnants of the ice his blood had temporarily frozen into when he'd been told of the accident.

She thought his basic human concern for another person's well-being was down to his 'love' for her, and he turned his face away so she wouldn't see his revulsion, at her and at himself, and dredged his parents and sister into his mind's eye. They were the people he needed to keep at the forefront of his thinking whenever the urge to rip off the mask of his deception became unbearable. Them and the thousands of Antoniadis Shipping employees. All those futures in his hands.

Turning his stare back to her, he smiled and held out one of the hands all those futures depended on.

There was only a small hesitation before her beautiful heart-shaped lips pulled into a shy smile and one of the tiny hands all those futures also depended on slipped into his and her fingers tentatively closed around his.

For the beat of a moment, he experienced the strangest sensation; the sensation of Lucie's fingers closing around his heart.

# CHAPTER FOUR

FOR ALL THAT Lucie had said only her head hurt, there was a stiffness to her gait evident when they made the short walk along the harbour with the nurse who'd accompanied them from the hospital.

Keeping a supportive grip on her hand, like any supportive fiancé would, Thanasis shortened his usual stride to keep pace with her. There was something about her tentative but determined steps that highlighted her current fragility and tugged at his chest. For the first time since she'd walked into the hotel bar he was wholly aware of how tiny and delicate she really was. Only her determination hinted at the combative personality he'd spent two months sparring and clashing with.

The medics who'd attended the scene of the accident had said it was nothing short of a miracle that she'd escaped the wreckage with nothing more than a bleeding nose from the airbag. Those medics didn't know how tough Lucie was. Thanasis could well imagine his car crumpling around her and then having second thoughts. The injury to her head had come about, so witnesses had attested, when she'd caught her foot stumbling out of the car. She'd been too disoriented by the accident to put her hands out to break her fall. It was nothing but bad luck that her head had landed on the edge of the pavement kerb.

He couldn't bring himself to think of her head hitting the kerb as being his good luck, even if he was using her amnesia to his full advantage.

When they reached his yacht, she stared at it for a long time, silently taking it all in. '*Persephone*... Is she where your island gets its name?'

'Yes. My island was inhabited many millennia ago and all that's known of the islanders is that they worshipped Persephone—there are ruins of a monument to her on the south of the island—which is where the island's name comes from. It seemed fitting to name my yacht after her too.'

'Wasn't she Queen of the dead or something?' Lucie asked dubiously, thinking the last person she'd name a yacht after was someone who represented death.

'Queen of the underworld, but she was much more than that. Hades was the god of the underworld and stole Persephone from her mother to live as his wife there with him, breaking Demeter's heart. Demeter was the goddess of harvest and fertility,' he explained. 'After much bad blood, Zeus decided Persephone would spend six months each year living with Hades and six months living with Demeter. The months with Hades were months of desolation where the land became barren and nothing grew because Demeter's heart was so desolate, but the months Persephone returned to her mother were months where

Demeter's happiness shone on the earth and blessed the land with an abundance of fertility, the months we know of as spring and summer.'

Her stare still glued to the yacht she was about to embark, a shiver ran up Lucie's spine. For a split moment certainty gripped her that this was all a trick and she was about to be stolen away just like Persephone had been.

And then she felt the comforting solidity of Thanasis's hand clasped around hers and shook the feeling away. Her mother would never win any parenting award but even she wouldn't send her daughter off to a remote island with a man to be stolen away. In any case, there would be other people on the island, household staff— she didn't imagine Thanasis had ever lifted a domestic finger in his life—along with all the people setting up for the wedding. And until they reached it, there was the crew of his yacht, a handful waiting patiently in identical uniforms of navy polo shirts and black shorts on the front deck for them to climb on board.

Most of all though, was Thanasis himself, and the intuition that had been in her since she'd first come round after the accident that he'd become a major part of her life. That they meant something to each other.

Thanasis's yacht, Lucie had to admit, was a lot classier than Georgios's. Georgios's yacht, a vessel she'd spent many of the long weeks of school summer holidays on, was a real party palace with everything geared around all ages having fun. Thanasis's, by contrast, brought to mind an ultra-luxurious spa with everything designed to aid relaxation, and she spent the six-hour journey to Sephone doing just that, mostly because she wasn't allowed to do anything else. In Lucie's case, relaxing meant sleeping, but that had nothing to do with the *Persephone*'s ambiance but was because of her jailers.

When Thanasis had said he wanted to ensure all her medical needs were taken care of, she hadn't thought he'd meant turning a cabin of the *Persephone* into a hospital room with a doctor and two nurses in attendance for good measure. The cabin had a private balcony the strict medics grudgingly allowed her to sit out on, but she wasn't allowed to stray any further.

Being so restricted meant boredom kicked in quickly, and while she'd slept enough for England and Greece combined these last five days, she ended up sleeping because there was absolutely nothing else for her usually active brain to do. She had no phone, no books to read and, having never been one for sitting down to watch films and binge on boxsets, no interest in her cabin's television. Waking to be told by a nurse that they were minutes away from the island had her scrambling out of bed with an agility that was close to feeling normal. She was certain her earlier stiffness had come from her muscles not being used for days.

Released from her cabin, she was escorted by her jailers to a saloon with the same calming opulence that permeated the rest of what she'd seen of the yacht.

Thanasis, standing with his back turned at the far end of the saloon with a clear view of the nearing island, was discussing something with a member of his crew. There was something strange about his posture, but it wasn't until he sensed or heard her presence and turned his head and the animation on his face fell and his hands dropped to his sides that she realised what the strangeness was. He'd been gesticulating.

Gesticulations were nothing out of the ordinary for the Greeks—in Lucie's considerable experience, being expressive was part of the national DNA—but they were definitely out of the ordinary for the rigidly composed Thanasis.

There was a barely perceptible narrowing of his eyes and rising of his broad shoulders before his features re-laxed and he headed towards her.

The same shiver of fear that had caught Lucie before she boarded the *Persephone* snaked freshly up her spine and stopped her feet moving forwards to him.

She didn't know this man.

Her bruised brain and Thanasis's ridiculously gor-geous face and wondrous scent had bamboozled her into believing that she knew him, but she didn't. He'd been hiding himself from her, and because of that, she couldn't read him. She didn't doubt her intuition that they meant something to each other but what was that *something* if he wouldn't let himself relax around her? How could she trust that *something* was a good something? It was absolutely in her mother's interest for the wedding to go ahead. It was absolutely in Thanasis's interest too. In fact, the only person in whose interest it wasn't was her. Or hadn't been. Lucie had led a fully independent life since finishing secondary school but the great job she'd adored and the funky flat she'd shared with three of her best friends were all gone. That all had to be the truth or why else would she be in Greece in July? No, make that August now.

He was only feet away from her.

Her heart thumped harder as his magnetic effect danced into her senses.

She was being irrational. What reason could Thanasis or her mother have to lie to her? She'd agreed to a marriage of convenience with him to save both families, so why embellish that?

He stopped before her and, his wondrous scent bamboozling her all over again, she suddenly realised just how big he really was, much more than she'd imagined from her hospital bed. He didn't just top her five foot nothing height but *towered* over it. The top of her head barely reached his shoulder and that included her untameable mass of hair.

'Good rest?' he asked, his stare as serious and intense as ever.

Matching his intensity, trying without any success to see into his head, she nodded. 'I think that was the most comfortable prison I've ever slept in.'

His forehead creased. 'Prison?'

'While you were having fun in the sun, my jailers refused to let me leave the cabin.'

'I asked them to watch you closely.'

'Did you impress upon them the need to watch me excessively closely?'

'Of course.' He folded his arms across his chest, biceps and pecs flexing with the movement. 'You have suffered a nasty head injury and I make no apologies for wanting your recovery to be as smooth as it can be. If it is any consolation, I was working, not having fun,' he added.

Trying very hard to concentrate on their conversation and not the swirl of dark hair visible through the opened throat of his black shirt, trying without any success to stop herself imagining those muscular arms enveloping her, Lucie lifted her chin and smiled sweetly. 'No consolation at all. I find my work immensely fun.'

'Then you, *matia mou*, are an anomaly. Work for me is work.'

'Poor you, but if you want my recovery to be smooth, I suggest you rethink any plans you might have dreamed up of locking me away until our wedding day while you get on with your non-exciting work, otherwise you'll find the wedding having to be postponed on account of me jumping out of a window and probably breaking my legs.'

There was another crease in his brow before his features loosened and he gave a short burst of laughter.

The only creases on his face now the lines around his eyes, he folded his arms and tilted his head. 'Consider your comment noted.'

Absurdly thrilled at the sound of his laughter, probably because if she'd had to put money on it she'd have said his vocal cords didn't stretch to laughing, Lucie mimicked his stance and riposted, 'Consider your consideration of my comment noted.'

The amusement on his face lasting longer than any of

his previous smiles, he inclined his head towards a door leading outside. 'Now that we have noted each other's comments, shall we go on deck so you can see your home for the next few weeks?'

Lucie's home for the next few weeks—there were plans for them to stay on Sephone a week after the wedding too, for their honeymoon—was the most stunningly beautiful place she'd ever seen. Even before the yacht had moored she understood exactly why Thanasis had chosen this particular island as his private hideaway.

Sephone rose from the crystal-clear blue waters of the Aegean like the majestic goddess it was named after, the mountainous terrain thick with vineyards and olives groves, sheer drops creating coves where the sea lapped onto some of the palest, softest-looking sand she'd ever seen.

Travelling with Thanasis by golf buggy to the villa over a wide, snaking pathway that had to be manmade but seemed as natural as the sweet-smelling flowers lining it, Lucie breathed in the pure air with a sense of wonder she didn't think she'd ever experienced before, and then she caught her first glimpse of the villa and nearly overdosed on it.

Nestled above a hidden cove with waters of the palest blue, multiple white domes with blue-domed roofs of varying sizes connected to create one palatial wonder amassed with an abundance of arched and circular windows, all blending into something not only beautiful but sensual, as if the architect had eschewed anything that could be construed as a straight line. It was like nothing she'd seen before, a home any goddess would be proud to inhabit.

'Who designed *this*?' she asked, close to breathless with admiration.

'Thomas Breakwell.'

'No way. *Thomas* designed this?'

Although she was too busy gaping at the stunning villa, she felt Thanasis's stare fall on her. 'You know him?'

'He hired our company to do the interiors for the showrooms of his apartment complex in Canary Wharf. I would never have guessed this was one of his.'

'I put the tender out with the vision of what I wanted. He was the architect who most understood the feel of what I was seeking.'

'Good for him…although now I'm wondering how come I didn't know of it.' At Thanasis's questioning stare, she explained, 'When we were pitching for the Canary Wharf project, Kelly got me to trawl through his company website. There is no way I would have forgotten this…' Her spirits suddenly plummeted. 'Unless there's more holes we didn't know about in my memories?'

'You wouldn't have seen it on his website,' he assured her. 'The project was undertaken in secrecy.'

'How come?'

'I didn't want the world to know about the island. It only encourages tourists to try and find it.'

'Then why are we marrying here? From what Mum was saying, the whole world and their dogs are coming.'

'Sometimes it feels like that,' he admitted wryly. 'Sephone was chosen because it has the romantic feel we thought it necessary to portray when we marry. To work and soothe our business investors, our marriage needs to be believable.'

'So you're giving up your secret hideaway for the greater good?' The tourists he'd bought the island to escape from would soon be poring over maps trying to figure out where in the Aegean Sephone was located.

'Some sacrifices are worth making.'

'Is that what I said when I agreed to the marriage?'

'If I recall correctly, you said you expected a nomination to be given on your behalf to the Nobel Prize panel.'

Meeting his eye for the first time since they'd got into the golf buggy, she grinned even as her heart swelled. 'That definitely sounds like something I would say.'

Thanasis, knowing she wouldn't be smiling if she remembered the context of her comment, nonetheless curved his lips, and was saved from having to say anything further on the subject by their buggy coming to a stop in front of the huge semi-circular timber door.

Her Nobel Prize nomination comment had come at the end of their first meeting in the hotel bar. If he was remembering correctly—and his memory had never failed him before—her exact words, thrown at her stepbrother Alexis, had been, 'If I pull this off and convince the world I'm in love with that...' she'd glared at Thanasis '...*man*, and that everything between our two families is now all jolly hockey sticks and cream buns, then I'd better get a Nobel Prize nomination out of it.'

'Would you like a nomination for sainthood too?' Thanasis had asked acidly.

'Only if I manage not to kill you.'

There had been countless times after when a look alone from Lucie would have sufficed to kill him stone dead.

There was no look like that or any kind of glare on her face now. Colour had returned to the cheeks made pale by her injury and there was a lightness in her expression, as if this whole thing was one big adventure for her and he was the man joining her on it. It was much like the shine that had been in her eyes when she'd bounced into the hotel bar, before his coldness had wiped it clean away. Much like the shine he'd gleaned when their eyes had met across the room all those years ago, that long, unbidden moment that had captured them tightly enough that they'd both remembered it years later.

Lucie gazed around at the most stunning room she'd ever been in. It was like she'd stepped into an airy white cave carved into paradise. Light poured in from multiple angles, bathing the enormous bed in golden light. She let her stare linger on it only a second before her heart turned over and she hastily looked anywhere else.

She wasn't ready to think of sharing that bed with Thanasis, especially not when she could feel him watching her reaction to their room with that intensity she felt like a physical touch.

How were you supposed to behave around someone you were marrying in a week's time and who you'd already shared months of a life building a relationship with, but who you had no memories of? The few displays of affection Thanasis had shown while she'd been cocooned in hospital had felt natural and thrillingly wonderful, but she'd been doped up to her eyeballs on drugs. It all felt very different and real now she was back out in the real world with nothing in her system to pollute her feelings or reactions, and she wished there were an instruction manual available to help her navigate it all so it didn't feel quite so terrifying.

'Seriously, who was the interior designer for this? Because I want to kiss them,' she said brightly, going into jocular mode to cover the disquiet that felt like no disquiet she'd ever experienced before at being alone with Thanasis in a bedroom for the first time, even though she knew this wasn't the first time because he'd been at her hospital bedside all that time, but that had been completely different because it was a hospital room, and that was not forgetting—even though she *had* forgotten— that she'd been sharing a bedroom with him for weeks and weeks, and now even her thoughts were going haywire and were on the cusp of making her head explode. 'This is amazing.'

'Helena Tatopoulos.'

'Can you give me her number so I can ask for a job?' she said, only half in jest.

He gave the flash of a grin. 'After the wedding.'

'Invite her to it so I can badger her there.'

He adopted a stern expression. 'No business talk at the wedding.'

She made a pffting sound. 'But business is the whole *point* of the wedding.'

Laughing lowly, he reached out to smooth down one of her curls sticking up at the ceiling, and her heart went haywire to match her thoughts even though he wasn't really touching her, well, not any part of her that was living, because hair wasn't actually alive, was it?

'I am the last person to forget that.' He released the curl and stepped back. 'I will leave you to settle in. Does dinner in an hour work for you?'

'The sooner the better—I'm starving.' Or had been. Nerves had kicked in big time. Or what felt like nerves. Right behind Thanasis was the sprawling bed they'd be sharing and because her eyes were currently glued to his gorgeous face with a special focus on his full lips…oh, but the way they moved when he spoke sent her pulses as haywire as her heart and thoughts…the bed was in her peripheral vision, and with the way the falling sunlight shone through the multiple windows casting both Thanasis and the bed in its golden glow…

Soon, very soon, those full lips would press against hers in that very bed…

Oh, God, her efforts not to think of the bed she'd very soon be sharing with him had become a dismal failure because now it was all she could think of, and suddenly she realised that all the things she'd wondered about in her hospital bed would be wonders no more but her reality, that *this* was her reality, her and Thanasis, committed lovers, and as all these thoughts collided a glow began to build inside her, flutters of deep, pulsing warmth that had her clutching at the material of her dress around her stomach even though she didn't know what she was clutching it for.

'Good,' said the full lips containing such sensuous promise that she was now caught on a tightrope between yearning for them to just *kiss* her, and wanting to throw herself out of a window to escape a fear she didn't even understand. 'Make yourself comfortable. Everything's been unpacked for you but if anything's been forgotten or there's anything else you need, tell any member of staff. If they don't have it, they will get it couriered over. If you feel unwell, the medical team are based in the room to the right of yours—pressing the green switches by your bed and dressing table sends an alert directly to them. There is also a switch in your bathroom.'

Lucie nodded as if she'd been paying attention to his words and not lost in fascination and fear at the movement of his mouth, and then realised exactly what he'd said and blinked. 'Isn't this our room?'

The mouth she'd been lost in fascination with twitched. 'No, *matia mou*, this is your room. My room is to your left.'

Her heart and stomach shrank and plummeted as full comprehension hit her. 'Oh, I thought…assumed…'

Assumed this was *their* room, words that went unsaid but which still echoed between the walls and between them.

Although Thanasis didn't move—how could someone so big be so *still*?—she sensed a shift within him, sensed him again reining in his composure to give nothing of himself away, and yet somehow the intensity of his stare increased, giving the sensation that he was searching inside all the compartments in her brain and plucking out the files hidden from herself and reading them.

'I am thinking only of you,' he murmured. 'The reset between us that's come about because of your injury...' Exhaling through his nose, he closed the distance he'd created between them and gently captured her chin. The probing green eyes beginning to swirl. 'I know you feel obliged to marry me, *matia mou*, but the last thing I want is for you to feel any other kind of obligation. That would be unconscionable of me.'

Heart caught in her throat, trembling inside and out and captured in a stare she couldn't have pulled herself away from if she'd tried, Lucie held her breath as the mouth she ached to feel closed in on hers.

The warmth of his breath danced over her lips and then the soft and yet, oh, so firm mouth brushed over hers in a lingering featherlight caress that left her close to sagging with disappointment when he pulled away from it.

Catching a locket of her hair, he rubbed the tip of his nose against hers. 'Let us be on an equal footing and start over as if we were both strangers to each other, and take our time in getting to know each other without any pressure or expectation.' With a glimmering smile, he brushed another featherlight kiss to her mouth and huskily added, 'There is no need to rush anything. I can wait for as long as you need me to, and I know the wait will be worth it because we have our whole life together to look forward to.'

And then he released the curl and stepped back, stealing the warmth she'd been barely aware of bathing in, leaving Lucie gaping at him, the fleeting kiss having struck her dumb,

'Until dinner, *matia mou*,' he whispered.

By the time she came back to her senses, Thanasis had disappeared from the room leaving her with the sense that she'd just been hypnotised as effectively as a cobra would be by a master snake charmer.

# CHAPTER FIVE

SEPHONE WAS THE one place Thanasis had ever felt a true sense of peace. Growing up, life had always been busy even during times of relaxation. Each evening, the family had congregated around the dining table to feast on the delicious food cooked fresh by the staff; grandparents, aunts, uncles and cousins frequent guests at the table along with numerous workers and business associates his generous parents would invite to break bread with them. The business had been central to Antoniadis life, an extension of their family, and it had always felt like Thanasis's family to him. He would never say it had been his destiny to one day run it, but it had never crossed his mind to do anything else.

It would never have crossed his mind to purchase his own island either, if he hadn't visited his friend Leander's island for a weekend of partying and found himself struck with the solitude one early morning while everyone else slept off the night before's excess. By the time the others started surfacing, he'd already determined to buy his own island and create a sanctuary for himself. Within two years, his sanctuary had been found and bought and the domed villa designed and built. It had been worth every cent of the vast sum spent on it, something his family and close friends agreed with as they all made liberal use of it too.

This was Thanasis's first visit to his sanctuary since the press had first splashed on just how toxic and dangerous the rivalry between his father and Georgios Tsaliki had become. He'd been in damage limitation mode ever since, barely coming up for air as he'd juggled investor concerns with stepping into his father's shoes and keeping an eye on his immediate family who were all suffering under the enormous strain of it all. And then there had been his need to be publicly visible with his new 'fiancée' to cement the idea of their 'love'.

It was the presence of his 'fiancée' that had stopped his lungs opening wide as he'd stepped off the *Persephone* and stopped the long exhalation that usually followed as all the pressures of his life lifted from his shoulders. The knowledge, too, that at the rear of the villa an army of people were transforming his landscaped garden into a wedding venue and that, dotted around the island, luxury yurts were being put up to accommodate the guests who wouldn't be travelling to the island on their own yachts and who there wasn't the room to accommodate in the villa.

But mostly it was Lucie herself. He'd never been able to breathe properly in her company. Always that cramped tightness in his chest, and as he did his best to compose himself in anticipation of her joining him at the poolside dining area, he took a long drink of his wine in another effort to wipe the taste of her from his mouth, and closed his eyes to wipe the image of her face as he'd last seen it.

She'd been as affected by those two barely-there kisses as he'd been.

Damn it.

Those two kisses had been too fleeting for any of Lucie's essence to seep into him but seep into him she had, a dark sweetness of breath that lingered, and he drained his wine, glancing at his watch. Two more minutes and she would be with him and he would have to pull himself together and carry on with the charade.

He'd had to kiss her. He'd read her surprise at their separate rooms. Read too her relief…and that flare of disappointment. He'd needed to placate her and stop doubts about their relationship fermenting, and he'd done it successfully. He should be in self-congratulatory mode because this was how it had to be, something he grimly reminded himself of as he refilled his glass. Whatever vulnerabilities Lucie might currently be suffering, that didn't change that this whole situation was of *her* making. She was the one who'd refused to listen, hadn't even let him explain. She'd seen what she'd wanted to see because it had suited her. She'd wanted out of their agreement and had run at the first opportunity, something else he needed to remind himself of if guilt at how he was playing her should bite a little too sharply.

She hadn't officially ended the engagement. That was yet another thing to remind himself of. As far as he knew—and he hoped like hell that his gut was correct on this—she had confided nothing about ending their engagement with anyone. For all he knew, if she hadn't crashed his car she might have let off all her steam thrashing it around and then come back home, thrown her Medusa glare at him, thrown some more choice insults at him and then carried on as if nothing had happened. God alone knew they'd had enough white-cold rages between them that had ended in that way. Always there had been the unspoken agreement that whatever their personal feelings for each other, their respective families and businesses were bigger than those feelings. It was the only thing apart from their mutual loathing of the press that they'd ever agreed on.

Some internal antennae lifted a moment before the bespoke French doors slid open and Lucie stepped out onto the patio.

The sun was giving its last goodbyes for the evening but even with little natural light to see by, he noted the slash of colour stain her cheeks as their eyes met.

She bit into her bottom lip and tentatively raised a hand. 'Hi.'

The beats of his heart strangely weighty, he exhaled slowly before rising to his feet. *Theos*, she looked stunning.

*'Kalispera, matia mou.'*

The beautiful smile she'd spent two months determinedly not bestowing on him lit her face, and she walked to the table, the stiffness of earlier much lessened. It wouldn't be long, he judged, before the bounce in Lucie's gait returned and she returned to full, glowing health.

She'd changed into another of her favoured black

dresses, a strapless, floaty number that perfectly suited her tiny, slender frame. Her black, curly hair had been piled on top of her head in the style he so loathed because he was incapable of looking at it and not wanting to pull out the clip holding it together just to watch it all tumble down. When she slipped into the chair he held out for her, he wasn't quick enough to stop his face twisting in fresh loathing as the scent of her perfume engulfed his senses.

Thanasis despised all of Lucie's perfumes but this was the one he'd once considered stealing out of her bedroom and incinerating. Only his absolute refusal to enter her private space had stopped him acting on this urge.

This was the perfume, more than all the others, that amplified her natural scent and gave off a sensuous, musky aroma that made him want to bury his face into her neck to inhale it deep into his lungs. It was the scent that turned sexual awareness into a charge so strong that he became unable to stop all the heady fantasies hovering beneath his consciousness from rising up and tormenting him with their vividness.

It was the perfume that turned his hunger into a craving.

Lucie had barely taken her seat before two members of staff appeared with a variety of mezes for them to dive into. While they fussed over both her and the table, placing the dishes into a perfect diamond formation between her and Thanasis whilst pouring her water and offering her a variety of alcoholic drinks that she thought it best to refuse considering the current state of her head, Lucie took the opportunity to regain the composure that had come within a whisker of being blown to smithereens with one look at Thanasis.

Heavens help her, he *did* something to her, and in less than a week she was going to be married to him. In a life she had no memory of, they'd made plans to spend the rest of their lives together, and all she really knew about him was what he'd chosen to show her, and all she really knew for certain about *them* was that her pulses were still racing and lips still tingling from those fleeting kisses barely an hour before.

But she had learned something concrete about him that day. She'd learned he was a gentleman. You only had to look at him…although she wasn't quite certain how looking at him allowed her to determine this…to know he was a highly sexual being. Despite Thanasis practically oozing testosterone and sexuality, he'd guessed that she'd geared herself up for sharing his bed and guessed too how frightening a prospect it had been for her, what with him being a stranger to her, and so had reset things between them to put them on an equal footing. So that made him a gentleman, and it made him empathetic. More proof, not that it was needed, that he wasn't the monster she'd been raised to believe him to be.

Could that be the reason for his rigidity around her? she suddenly wondered. While he was understanding of the loss of her memories, he still had his own, and she took a moment to put herself in his shoes. If their roles were reversed and she was the one who had not only all the memories of their time together but all the feelings too…

To unexpectedly find mutual love with someone and then find that person's love for you had been wiped out as if it had never occurred? Oh, but it must be one of the most awful things in the world.

'Are you okay?'

Thanasis's voice pulled her out of her latest batch of rambling thoughts.

The intense green eyes were watching her closely.

'You looked lost in your thoughts,' he said with a half-smile.

She couldn't help but smile at how unerringly accurate this observation was, even as her chest filled with a fizzing emotion for this stranger who knew her so, so well.

'I was thinking about you,' she admitted.

He raised an eyebrow in question.

'I was thinking how hard this whole situation must be for you. I don't know how I'd cope if I were in your shoes.'

Pale green gaze boring into her, he said, 'All that matters is that you are here, and if having you here means you and me starting over then that is better than any alternative.'

The fizzing in her chest spread up and into her throat, and suddenly she recognised truth and sincerity in his stare, the first time she'd been able to accurately read him at all, and the relief that came with this reacted to the fizzing in her chest and throat, and shot out of her mouth as a burst of joyful laughter.

Bemusement playing on his dreamy face, now both of his dark eyebrows rose in question.

She leaned forwards. 'I know I've thanked you before, but I'm going to thank you again, for being there for me while I was in hospital and for being here for me now, and for all the accommodations you're making for me. Thank you.'

The guilt that lanced Thanasis's guts at this was so sharp and unexpected that it took him a moment to respond. 'It is nothing you wouldn't do for me,' he lied.

But he hadn't lied about Lucie being here being all that mattered. That was the greatest truth of all because the alternative was the destruction of everything and everyone he cared about, and the destruction of everything and everyone she cared about too. When the truth was revealed after the wedding, he would make her understand the lies were for both their benefit.

Her black eyes shining, her heart-shaped lips pulled into a smile softer than he'd ever have imagined Lucie Burton capable of pulling. 'I'm starting to believe that.'

Internal alarms ringing at the direction Lucie was steering the conversation—there were lies and then there were damned lies—Thanasis straightened his spine and pulled a smile of his own. 'Eat, *matia mou*. My chefs have been busy creating all your favourite dishes.'

One thing he had learned through all their torturous meals out together was that Lucie had a particular addiction to cheese. All cheeses. And so it came as no surprise at all when she loaded her plate with keftedes, Kalamata olives, sliced vine tomatoes and tzatziki, and sprinkled what had to be half a block of crumbled feta over the whole lot of it before happily diving in.

At her first bite of the keftedes, her already shining eyes shone even brighter. 'Wow,' she said once she'd swallowed it. 'These are amazing. Forget falling in love and all that business stuff—I'd marry you for your chef.'

He couldn't help but laugh, even as he remembered her once telling him the only worthwhile thing in his whole rotten life was his head chef. That had come off the back of Thanasis icily telling her when she'd unexpectedly joined him for dinner in his apartment, that he preferred to dine alone than have his meal spoilt by her presence. He would eat with her in public as part of the whole performance but in the privacy of his apartment, he wanted solitude. Unfortunately, solitude and Lucie did not go together. Her husky voice followed him everywhere, even when he was on the other side of the four thousand square metre space from her. The bounce of her footsteps echoed through the walls. There were nights when he swore he could hear her breaths of sleep.

'Let's play a game,' she said once she'd demolished her first course and was steadily working through their main course of spanakopita—another Lucie favourite—served with roasted vegetables.

'What kind of game?'

She stabbed her fork into a mound of roasted aubergines and peppers. 'Getting to Know You. We play it at work with all the newbies, but obviously, as it's just the two of us, we'll have to adapt it. It's literally a game of asking each other questions that allow you to get to know someone better.'

'What kind of questions?'

'Any kind. Favourite colour. Favourite film. First kiss. What car you learned to drive in. Anything, really. The only rule is no closed questions or answers—basically, nothing that can be answered with a yes or no, oh, and as you already know me and I'm the one with the big memory hole, I think it's only fair that I get to ask you three questions to each one of yours.' She popped the fork into her mouth.

That worked for him. He didn't want to get to know Lucie any better than he already did, and, watching her devouring her food, said, 'Where do you put it all?' It was one of the many questions that had built up during their two-month engagement. Their tortured public meals together had been spent with fake smiles, fake conversation, and Lucie eating everything put in front of her and more.

She caught his eye and grinned. 'Is that your first question?'

'I suppose it must be.' A nice, neutral question that would reveal little to nothing about her.

'I have a fast metabolism, but you must already know that.'

'I know you have more energy than the average person.'

'I just get bored sitting around and doing nothing, that's all. Maybe that does help with my metabolism, but seeing as I inherited it from my mum and she'd be happy spending her whole life on a sun bed, I don't think that's the full explanation for it. My turn—when's your birthday?'

'February the nineteenth.'

'Ah, so that must make you a Pisces.'

'I believe so… Do you believe in that stuff?' For all the dark, bohemian flow of the clothes she wore, this surprised him.

'Not in the slightest, but I went through a phase when I was fourteen of obsessing over it and wanting to know everyone's star sign, and the nosey part of me still likes to know. So, Pisces is a water sign… You like swimming?'

'No.'

'Closed answer.'

'It was a closed question.'

'Fair enough. I'll rephrase it—why don't you like swimming, and, seeing as you don't like it, why on earth do you have a swimming pool?'

'I don't like swimming because I nearly drowned as a child. I have a swimming pool because my friends and family like to make use of the island and they all like to swim.'

'Oh, blimey, that sounds terrible,' she said, clearly shocked. 'How old were you? What happened?'

'That is another two questions.'

'No, they're follow-ons because you didn't answer fully.'

He shook his head in mock disappointment. 'You didn't say that was in the rules.'

She fluttered her eyelashes. 'I forgot. I'm telling you it now.'

He laughed at her chutzpah. 'I dive-bombed into the pool when I was four. I couldn't swim and didn't realise the danger of what I was doing. One of the gardeners pulled me out—I was lucky that he was pruning the pool-side flowers and heard the splash I made. I suffered no long-term trauma other than a dislike of my face being submerged. I did learn to swim, just to prove to myself that I could do it, but I've never taken any enjoyment in it. Is that a satisfactory answer for you?'

Her eyes narrowed. 'Hmm…' And then she gave a decisive nod. 'Yes, that'll do. Moving on, what—?'

'You've had your three questions,' he interrupted.

'No, I haven't.'

'Yes, you have. Birthday, whether I like swimming and why I have a swimming pool.'

She pouted in mock outrage. 'No fair—the two swimming ones were linked.'

'Linked but separate, which means it's now my turn.'

Her scowl was completely negated by the glee in her eyes.

'When was the first time you got drunk?' he asked as she dug into a thick slice of sticky walnut cake he couldn't even remember being put in front of her. There was a slice in front of him too. He had only the vaguest recollection of their main course being cleared away.

'When I was fifteen. I would like to point out that it was also the last time I got drunk.'

'Elaborate,' he commanded.

She spooned another huge mouthful of cake into her mouth. After swallowing it, she gave a dreamy sigh. 'Would you object to me snogging your chef? Because this is seriously good cake.'

'And you always "snog" people who make good cakes?'

'Never had the urge before, but this is seriously, seriously good. I bet they serve this on Mount Olympus... that is where the Greek gods live, isn't it?'

'Correct.'

'I'd lock your chef up in case Jupiter tries to nab him from you.'

'I think you mean Zeus—Jupiter was a Roman god.'

She shoved another spoonful of cake into her mouth with a this-cake-is-far-too-good-for-me-to-care shrug.

'But I will be sure to pass your compliments to Elias... and pass on your wish to "snog" him.'

Chewing contentedly, she stuck a thumb up.

'In the interests of employer and employee relations, I should warn you that if he objects to being objectified for his cake-making skills, then I will have to put the brakes on any form of "snog" or we run the risk of him leaving and never making another cake for you again.'

Eyes wide with alarm, she spooned in yet more of her rapidly disappearing cake and frantically shook her head.

'But if he agrees to your objectification, then a "snog" will be fine. Out of curiosity, will there be tongues involved?'

She frowned and shook her head again, turning her thumb down for good measure.

'*Kalos*. And now that that is resolved, you can elaborate on your one and only drunken escapade.'

She made him wait until she'd finished the last of her cake before answering. He didn't mind. Watching Lucie devour every last crumb had an erotic appeal that evoked fantasies about taking a masterclass in sticky walnut cake making and then spooning it into that delicious mouth himself.

*Theos*, the joy she took from food was something else. He could watch her eat all night. Watch those perfect heart-shaped lips...

'Athena stole a whole bottle of ouzo from her dad and the two of us thought it a brilliant idea to drink shots of it until the bottle was empty,' she finally said, cutting through his wayward fantasies. 'Alexis and Constantine found us in the garden and had to carry us to bed because neither of us was capable of walking...' Her voice trailed off, eyes narrowing again but this time with concern. 'What's wrong?'

Thanasis drained the last of his wine and shook his head. 'Nothing. Just trying to picture the scene.'

'It wasn't a pretty one,' she admitted, features loosening a touch, as if only half convinced by his explanation.

He could hardly tell her the truth, that the moment Athena's name had come out of Lucie's mouth, the erotically charged lightness of his mood had extinguished.

He'd forgotten who he was talking to. Forgotten why he was there. Why they were there.

For a few brief moments Lucie had stopped being Lucie Burton, stepdaughter of Georgios Tsaliki and daughter of Rebecca Tsaliki, and just been the beautiful, sexy, amusing woman sitting across the table from him sharing a delicious and increasingly flirtatious meal in the warm open air.

Their first meal alone together with no public watching them and he'd got caught in a moment he'd spent two months fighting tooth and nail to never be captured in.

He had to clear his tightened throat to ask the most natural follow-on question. 'You got into trouble for it?'

'Nope. It was put down to teenage high jinks, plus I think the general feeling was our hangovers were a worthy punishment—honestly, we were both as sick as dogs the next day.'

'I'm not surprised,' he murmured.

She grinned. 'I well and truly learned my lesson from it. Athena didn't though, but never mind, I'm sure she'll learn it one day. Anyway, my turn to ask a question.'

'Tomorrow.'

Her face fell.

*Theos*, he had to fight to make his voice sound normal. 'The medical team need to do all their checks on you.'

'But I feel fine,' she protested.

'I know, but for my peace of mind, I would like you to let them do their job. You've suffered a significant head wound, *matia mou*—you were only discharged this morning into my care on the promise that you would take things easy.'

She eyed him in silence for the longest time before giving a slow nod. 'Okay, I'll be a good girl and go to my room and let the medical team poke and prod me, but only for tonight. From tomorrow, I'm in charge of my own care.'

His heart nearly thumped out of his ribs when she reached across the table to cover his hand.

Her voice softening to match the softness in her black eyes, she said, 'I know your heart's in the right place and I can only imagine how hard these last few days have been for you, but I don't need or want you to make decisions for me. I've lived independently since I was eighteen, answerable to no one but myself. I'm not a child, Thanasis, so please don't treat me like one.'

He looked down at their joined hands with thick blood roaring in his ears. The sensation of Lucie's skin against his was like being marked by Aphrodite, the goddess whose seductive charms few men could resist, and it was taking all his strength not to twist his hand and wrap his fingers around hers.

Too much wine, he thought dimly. It had seeped through his system to dismantle the guard he kept fully raised around her, and only when he was confident that he could look at her without losing the last of his guard did he raise his gaze and hoarsely say, 'Message received and understood.'

She smiled tremulously and moved her hand away, pressed her fingers to her mouth and then leaned forwards to press them to his lips. '*Kalinychta*, Thanasis.'

He could do nothing to stop his lips kissing the delicate fingers. *'Kalinychta, matia mou.'*

# CHAPTER SIX

ON HER FIRST morning in Sephone, Lucie woke to the rising sun and to the remnants of a dream where Athena had been cruelly laughing in a strange yet somehow familiar living room. The unsettled, almost sick feeling the dream had set off in her was countered by the lack of waking fuzziness in her head, and she climbed out of bed with the spring in her step that had been missing since the accident.

Making herself a coffee from the posh machine in her room, she was about to carry it through the arched glass door that led out to her balcony when a tap on her bedroom door stopped her in her tracks.

Her heart tripling the rate of its beats, a wide smile had formed before she opened the door, a smile that faltered when she found one of the nurses standing there and not the man who'd been lodged in her mind as she'd fallen asleep and still been firmly ensconced there when she'd woken. The nurse must have stayed awake all night with her ear to the adjoining wall listening out for movement.

After whispering refusals of painkillers and all the health checks that apparently were *still* completely necessary, and insisting she was completely fine, Lucie softly closed the door on the poor nurse and padded outside.

Just as the villa itself was uniquely beautiful, her balcony was too, gentle steps leading down to a comfortable seating area fronted by a narrow swimming pool that appeared to snake the entire upper perimeter in a touch of aesthetic genius, winding through the adjoining balcony to her left... Thanasis's sprawling balcony.

She only needed to think of his name for her pulses to go haywire.

Was he awake yet, an early riser like her, or was he like the majority of her step and half-siblings and a bear with a sore head if woken before midday? She'd caught a glimmer of the real Thanasis Antoniadis during the meal when he'd finally relaxed around her, and what she'd discovered had delighted her. He was on her wavelength! He hadn't taken her silly comment about wanting to snog his chef seriously but had played along with it and while this was just a silly, minor thing it meant so much because there was nothing worse than having to explain a throwaway jest, something Lucie had way too much experience with as her humour often went over people's heads, but Thanasis had got it and played along with it, and it had been wonderful.

Oh, but there were so many things to learn and discover about him, and she longed to knock on his door and continue all the learning and discovering, but it was too early for most humans to rise.

Close to giddy with anticipation for the day to begin, she decided to take a swim and hurried to her dressing room in search of a swimsuit, hoping whoever had packed for her had thought to pack beachwear.

Result!

Modest black one-piece squeezed into, she finished her coffee, grabbed a towel from her bathroom and bounded back outside.

Lowering herself into the cool water, trying especially hard not to give her usual squeak when the water level reached between her legs so as not to wake the rest of the household, soon she was at the pool's edge gazing over the clear blue Aegean and the islands dotted in the distance.

Thanasis really had found paradise here. She'd never known such stillness before. Always there was noise in her life. Always. Here on Sephone, she could hear the birds singing their early morning chorus and the only sound to cut through it was the gently lapping sea rather than never ending traffic. The air felt cleaner, the sky crisper... She sighed with the pleasure of it all. Bliss.

Time to see if the pool really did snake the whole perimeter, but which direction to take? The route that took her past the bossy medical team's room or the one past Thanasis's? Decisions, decisions. She had the strong feeling that if either caught her, she'd meet disapproval, what with her 'condition' and all that. With at least one member of the medical team already awake and Thanasis likely still sleeping, her choice was made.

Swimming her preferred breaststroke, she set off with slow, lazy movements and made a studious effort not to turn her head to peek into Thanasis's room. Her peripheral vision showed that his balcony was vastly bigger than hers, the far end formed of its own half-dome with panoramic views that provided shelter from both the sun and the minimal rain the island was subjected to.

The pool wound round, intermittent narrow bridges to swim under and a new vista for her eyes to feast on of high rugged terrains and the undulating verdant greens of the island's olive groves and vineyards, and then she rounded yet another bend to the rear of the villa and hooked her arms over the pool's edge to take it all in.

Dinner had been eaten at the main poolside's dining area. She could just about make it out from her vantage point, but what she could see clearly now and had failed to notice the night before was the sensational sprawling grounds that had to be Thanasis's garden. He must have used a landscape gardener of equal renown to his architect, she thought, awed at what had been created out of nothing and so cleverly and sympathetically designed that unless you knew better you'd assume you'd fallen into the Garden of Eden. This Garden of Eden had a giant marquee in its centre and hiding just behind it—although she knew it was an illusion and really it was situated a long way behind it—a solitary domed white chapel, identifiable by the giant cross sticking out of its white roof.

Her airwaves suddenly tightened, white noise filling her ears in a rush.

That chapel had to be where she and Thanasis would marry. That marquee had to be where they would host their wedding reception. And those sleepy-looking workmen traipsing across the lawn carrying long poles over their shoulders had to be part of the crew tasked with transforming the garden into a fairy-tale wedding venue designed to convince the whole world that the bride and groom were destined to live happily ever after.

Their marriage was no abstract thing. It was real. In less than a week she would be a married woman and she had absolutely no idea if the sudden rabid fluttering in her stomach was an indication of excitement or terror.

'Please, tell me I am hallucinating.'

Still struggling to breathe, Lucie whipped her head round. Finding Thanasis by the side of the pool, all tousle-haired and stubble-faced and wearing a pair of baggy canvas shorts, made the struggle a whole lot worse.

He could have stepped off Mount Olympus for an early morning walk with the mortals.

*Back off, Adonis*, she thought dimly. *Your replacement has arrived.*

Adonis would take one look at Thanasis and retire on the spot.

She'd known he had a great body but even her vivid imagination had failed to paint it in all its glory. Thanasis had the broad muscularity gym bunnies around the world worked their socks off to sculpt their bodies into, but there was none of the bulging veins Lucie's nose always wrinkled at. Instead, it was as if Mother Nature herself had decided to bless him with perfection, from the deep olive hue of his skin to the smattering of fine dark hair that covered his defined chest and abdomen.

Dear heavens, had there ever been a finer specimen of manhood in the history of the world? This was the man who in a few short days she would exchange vows with and pledge to spend the rest of her life with, and as all these thoughts tumbled in her healing brain and her pulses throbbed just to look at him, she understood the fluttering in her stomach contained not an ounce of fear.

This gorgeous, sexy man was her fiancé and he was in love with her, and last night she'd finally understood for the first time since waking in her hospital bed why she'd fallen in love with him in turn.

The full lips she'd been dreaming of as she'd fallen into her real dreams tightened. Folding his arms, he repeated in clipped tones, 'Tell me I am hallucinating.'

She swam as close as she could get and held on to the poolside to look up at him. '*Kalimera* to you too.'

'Are you insane?' he said in the same clipped tone that contained strong undertones of anger. 'You have suffered a major head injury.'

'So you keep reminding me.'

'I shouldn't have to keep reminding you. Swimming alone in your condition is the height of insanity. Anything could have happened.'

'Erm…you know I can stand up in it, right? And I'm barely five foot.'

'That is not the point,' he virtually snarled. 'You have recklessly endangered yourself.'

She was still filled with all the fizz she'd set off on her swim with, Thanasis's appearance having added extra zing to it, and her good mood refused to dampen despite his obvious anger. 'Are you always this overbearing or is it just an early morning thing?'

'Over—?' His mouth snapped shut and he took a visible deep breath.

'Look,' she said before he could open his mouth again. 'I appreciate your concern, I really do, although quite honestly I'd prefer it without the headmaster tone, but as I told you last night, I'm not a child. I don't just feel fine today, I feel normal, like properly normal. There was no danger at all in me taking a swim... By the way, how did you know I was out here? I swam past your room ages ago.'

'This is the other side of my room,' he said tightly.

'Your room must be humungous.'

'It's big enough.' He took another deep breath. 'I know you think you are recovered but I gave my word to the medical team at the hospital that I would make you take things easy until the wedding.'

She couldn't help but smile at how visibly he was trying to rid himself of his visible anger. 'Poor you, thinking you could make me do anything.'

His jaw clenched and he raised his gaze to the heavens. 'This isn't a joke. I know you hate being told what to do but for once will you please just do as you're asked and keep yourself safe?'

Absurdly, this pleased her, yet more unneeded evidence that Thanasis really did know her and more unneeded evidence that he really did care for her, even if he did need to work on how he expressed that caring. She got it though. If the shoe were on the other foot and she were in love with him and saw him doing something she considered reckless then she'd probably be all over-protective too.

Sidestepping on the tips of her toes to the nearest gently inclining steps, Lucie got out of the pool and gave a mock curtsey. 'There. I'm being a good girl again, and if it makes you happy, I'll make a good girl promise not to go swimming on my own without supervision or arm bands until our wedding.'

Even though his eyes were still raised and his body language all tight and controlled, to her delight, his lips twitched as a glimmer of amusement flashed on his gorgeous face.

'And now that's all cleared up, do you have a towel I can use please?'

His neck rolled before he gave a sharp nod and turned to an inbuilt shelving unit stacked with towels and toiletries, and for the first time she noticed that this section of balcony didn't just have a long L-shaped sofa and coffee table but a Jacuzzi bath and an outside shower too.

Thanasis averted his eyes as he handed Lucie the towel. She was wearing what had to be the plainest, least revealing swimsuit he'd ever seen on a woman and yet his veins were as thick and heavy as they'd been when he'd caught that glimpse of her semi-naked in her hospital room.

He turned his face away so he wasn't subjected to the torture of watching her rub the towel over her delectable body. He needed to cool his core temperature, not raise it.

He should have bribed the doctors to keep her at the hospital a few more days.

After a night of restless sleep, which he'd given up on when the sun had risen, he'd thrown himself out of bed with a renewed determination to avoid Lucie's company as much as humanly possible... And then he'd glimpsed her swimming past his bedroom without a care in the world and clearly no care for the significant head trauma she'd suffered.

He'd come within a breath of bodily snatching her out of the water.

'Have you always been this rebellious?' he asked in a rougher tone than intended, but God help him he defied anyone in his shoes not to struggle containing their emotions when faced with someone who combined the beauty of Aphrodite with the discord strewn by Eris.

All the discord Lucie sowed lay entirely within him, and as Thanasis felt her stare fix on him and his awareness for her magnified, he thought she must have a touch of Hecate in her too. What else explained the growing sensation that he was being cast under a spell?

'I don't know about being rebellious,' she said musingly. 'I just know my own mind and have learned over the years how to assert it. I guess it was the whole growing up in two wildly different households thing.'

He made the mistake of looking at her.

She was bent forwards, drying her ankles, but those big black eyes were glued to his face. 'Sorry if you've already heard it all before—I'm guessing things are going to be like Groundhog Day for a while for you—but on the off chance I never shared my childhood with you, it was all pretty bonkers.'

She patted around her thighs... *Theos*, they were so exquisitely toned and slender...

'My dad's an accountant,' she explained, now drying her arms, 'and I spent the majority of my childhood living with him in a bog-standard ordinary house where everything was quiet and orderly and everything had its place and rules were strictly enforced, and then I'd spend the school holidays with Mum and Georgios and Athena and all the others, and life was just one big party and the only real rule was to *have fun*. Dad expected me to be dutiful and studious and grow up to be an accountant or a doctor, and Mum expected me to be glamorous—I distinctly remember her plucking my eyebrows when I was nine—and trade off my looks and attract a billionaire of my own like she'd done. I'd get off the plane in England and the first thing I'd have to do was wipe off the makeup Mum had trowelled on my face because Dad would have gone spare to see me wearing it. In their own ways, they both wanted to control me, but I guess I must have an in-built independent streak because I always knew I never wanted what either of them wanted for me.'

And this was why Thanasis had spent two months avoiding Lucie's company. He didn't want to know her, didn't want to have to think of his headstrong fiancée as anything but the woman she was today, most definitely didn't want to think of her as a child constantly yo-yoing between two households and countries, a square peg in a round hole in both of them, didn't want to hear anything from the husky voice that would knock at his defences and turn her into anything less than his enemy.

'What did you want?' he asked before he found the sense to end the conversation.

She shrugged and smiled and wrapped the towel around herself, and in the process wrapped the spell she was casting on him a little tighter too. 'To be free to live my own life and make my own choices. What about you? Did you ever want to do anything different from what your parents wanted for you…? I'm assuming your parents always wanted you to one day take over the running of Antoniadis Shipping?'

'They wanted it but they never put any pressure on me. If I'd chosen a different path, they would have been disappointed but they would have supported me.'

'Good for them. I got it in the neck from both my parents when I went straight into work from school. Dad wanted me to go to university and Mum wanted me to get a boob job. Oh, well, at least I've disappointed them equally so no one can accuse me of favouritism.'

'Your mother is a piece of work,' he said scathingly, an utterance and tone he regretted as soon as it left his mouth.

'She is who she is just as I am who I am,' Lucie said with a small lift of her shoulders that did nothing to hide the sadness flickering on her face. 'I will never be the daughter either of my parents wanted.'

Thanasis had to clench his jaw to stop himself placating her and pointing out that it was never a child's job to live up to parental expectations, that it was the parents' job to adjust those expectations to the individual child before them, just as his own parents had done with Lydia.

But none of this was any of his damned business. This was a conversation he should never have allowed to develop and he was damned if he was going to allow himself to feel empathy for a woman who'd given up the freedom she'd disappointed both parents by insisting on out of love and loyalty for the monster that was Georgios Tsaliki.

Time to extract himself from this situation.

Except there was no time to think of an excuse to rid himself of her, for Lucie, despite the towel wrapped around her hanging like a giant tent down to her feet, gracefully threw herself onto his outdoor sofa and with a smile said, 'Can we order some breakfast now, please? I'm starving.'

Why the hell had he gone along with this? Thanasis asked himself moodily as he watched yet another slice of *bougatsa* disappear into Lucie's delectable mouth. The wedding was only days away and there was no end of things that needed his approval, and that was without considering all the business stuff that needed his attention. A hundred ready-made excuses and he'd failed to conjure a single one.

'Do I get on with your family?' she asked, wiping her mouth with a finger and then licking the crumbs stuck to it.

He leaned across the coffee table to refill his coffee. It was getting to the stage where he'd rather dive into the main swimming pool than watch her eat. Anything than have to watch her eat. Each bite thickened the spell of awareness and the only way to break it was to escape her company altogether.

He needed to get out of here.

'It is too early to say,' he replied evasively.

'Ah, so they hate me.'

His gaze zipped back to her before he could stop himself.

She sighed and gave a rueful smile that shouldn't have tugged at his chest. 'Thank you for trying to spare my feelings but it really isn't necessary—I'd much rather have the truth even if it does hurt. I'm not a Tsaliki but I understand why they would see me as one, and I get why that would cloud their judgement of me.'

About to deny it, he closed his eyes briefly and nodded. Once they were married, Lucie would learn for herself the depth of his family's loathing of her and the entire clan of Tsalikis and hangers-on.

She gave another sigh and helped herself to what had to be her fourth slice of *bougatsa*. 'Oh, well, hopefully in time they'll see for themselves that I'm not the Antichrist and that the feud has nothing to do with me at all, and just accept me for myself like you did.'

He didn't want to hear this. He didn't want to hear or talk about *any* of this and put himself in a position where he had to tell the barefaced lies that were so necessary but that were becoming increasingly difficult to form.

Holding on to his loathing of Lucie had been a damn sight easier when the loathing had been mutual and she'd wanted to escape his presence as much as he'd wanted to escape hers. A damn sight easier when she wasn't half sprawled on his sofa with her pretty feet pointing at him, the towel having come loose and now lying half draped on the floor exposing her smooth legs, and with her beautiful face glued to his. Her hair drying in the rising sun was an untamed mass of curls pinging in all directions and damn if it didn't make her even sexier. Damn if the modesty of her swimsuit didn't make her sexier too, and it was taking everything he had not to let his eyes drift to the barest hint of cleavage on show.

It was like the forbidden fruit analogy but in flesh form, he thought, as he fought even harder against the awareness threading so heavily in his veins. The more flesh that was covered, the greater the desire to uncover it all. Most women's swimwear left so little to the imagination that you didn't need an imagination to know what lay beneath it. Not with Lucie. The bottom half of hers was more modest than the top half, wrapping around her skin like a pair of tight shorts and revealing not an inch of buttock…or anything else, and he could not stop himself from imagining what lay between those slender, succulent thighs. *Theos*, he kept inhaling that damned perfume even though he knew it was an impossibility and that not a trace of it remained on her golden flesh.

'What about you and my family?' his feminine temptation asked, bringing more *bougatsa* to her lips. 'I know I wasn't fit for much when I was in hospital but I don't think I imagined the tension between you and my mother.'

'Until you were hospitalised, the only members of

your family I'd had face-to-face contact with were Alexis and Athena.'

She chewed morosely before she brightened and sat up a little straighter while at the same time straightening her right leg.

Her toes were now barely an inch from his thigh. Sexy toes painted blood orange.

God help him, when had he ever found toes sexy? But Lucie's were. Pretty, sexy feet topped with pretty, sexy nails painted a colour filled with erotic imagery.

'Oh, well,' she said, clearly oblivious to the torture he was suffering, 'I suppose it's going to take time for the families to properly bury the hatchet.'

'There is not going to be any burying of any hatchet. Once we're married and the pictures of the two parties breaking bread together have been printed across the world, both families will return to their respective lives and go back to despising each other. The feud will be over on paper but not in hearts.' He said all this in as even a tone as he could manage, and then, using sheer force, wrenched his stare away from her sexy toes...

Only to land it straight onto her beautiful face at the same moment the tip of her moist, pink tongue darted out to catch a flaky crumb stuck in the corner of her exquisite mouth, and he found himself suppressing a groan as a wave of desire he could neither staunch nor deny to himself punched through him and his body twisted closer to her before he was even aware of what it was doing.

*Theos*, every inch of her was exquisite. Every damn inch. She didn't need to wear sexy clothes to be sexy or to spray perfume onto her skin to smell heavenly. She was Aphrodite, the goddess not just of beauty but of pleasure...of desire.

The eyebrows first plucked by her mother at the age of nine—what kind of mother did something like that? he wondered dimly—drew together as her gaze dipped to his mouth. 'Do you really believe that?'

He leaned closer still. 'Do you mean that you don't?' he whispered.

The black eyes flickered back up to meet his stare and widened. How had he never seen the flecks of gold in her eyes before, and now that he saw them, they were all he could see, tiny flecks of gold fire burning... hypnotising him.

Colour heightened her exquisite cheeks, the flecks of gold swirling. Her lips parted and she hitched a small breath. 'I...' She shook her head slowly, her voice barely audible even though her face was craning towards his. 'I don't know...but if you and I can...'

Her words tailed away as another thick throb of desire pulsed through him, all his senses soaking in the flawless beauty of the goddess who was drinking him in with the same dazed intensity with which he was drinking her.

He could smell the heat of her skin and the sweetness of her breath.

Barely aware of what he was doing, Thanasis wrapped his fingers around the warm, silken calf of her leg. A groan rose up his throat.

*Theos*, even her skin was flawless.

Her lips parted and released a quiet gasp, her wide eyes pulsed and her knee made the lightest of jerks.

That lightest of jerks was strong enough to snap him back to his senses, and in an instant he snatched his hand away and, heart pounding like a jackhammer, pulled his face away from the flawless beauty he'd been barely an inch away from kissing.

# CHAPTER SEVEN

LUCIE SHOOK HER head in a futile attempt to clear it of the blood rushing through it and sucked on lips that barely a moment ago had been alive with anticipation of Thanasis's kiss. She was trembling. Every part of her. Trembling and aching.

He rubbed a giant hand over his face and took a long breath.

Even through all the dazed sensations consuming her, Lucie had just enough wits left to recognise the torture Thanasis was putting himself through, and her ragged heart swelled at the control he must be continually exerting for her sake.

Pulling herself together as best she could, she shuffled over, closing the distance his sudden lurch away had created between them, and took hold of his hand. It stiffened at her touch.

The shutters were back in his eyes, his expression once again unreadable, and she gave a tremulous smile to see it…and to see the tic pulsing in his jaw.

On impulse, she scrambled unsteadily onto her knees and palmed his cheeks…her whole hands fitted on them,

the thick stubble brushing deliciously into her skin…
and brought her face even closer, dizzily breathing in
the scent of coffee lacing his breath.

'You don't have to walk on eggshells or treat me like
I'm breakable, Thanasis,' she whispered. 'My memories
of us might be gone but something of what we shared
must have imprinted in me because the feelings haven't.'

Something flashed in the green eyes before they
closed and his strong throat moved. 'Lucie, I…'

She slid her fingers over his mouth and shook her
head. 'You don't have to explain anything. I can see how
hard this whole situation is for you.' And then, because
she could do nothing else, she slipped her fingers away
from his lips and replaced them with her mouth.

If Thanasis had been still before, every muscle in his
powerful body now tensed, and as her eyes closed and
she sank into the sensations dancing over her mouth and
into her skin at the compression of the lips she couldn't
stop fantasising about against hers, the control he was exerting made her swollen heart expand to fill every crev-
ice inside her. Sighing into him, she slipped her hands
round to clasp the back of his head and slowly dragged
her fingers through hair softer than silk.

She sensed rather than heard the groan in his throat
before the unyielding mouth flexed and his lips parted,
only a fraction but fraction enough for his breath to fill
her senses with a taste and heat so delicious that her
brain shut down completely under the weight of sensation flooding her.

Thanasis could hear nothing above the roar in his

head, could barely hear his own urgent commands to resist, to unclasp the hands clinging so tightly to his head and push Lucie away before he gave in to the hunger and melted into her honeyed temptation.

He must not fall into it. He must resist. Resist, resist, resist, and with this one thought pushing through the growing cacophony in his brain, he lifted his hands with every intention of pushing her away but instead found his fingers cupping her face as his head tilted to fuse their mouths into one. The tips of their tongues collided and a burst of lust like he'd never experienced in the whole of his life smashed into him, its force so shocking that, with a hoarse groan, he buried his fingers into her mass of soft curls and opened his mouth to her.

Fire raging through his veins, his tongue swept into her hot, sweet temptation.

*Theos*, she tasted even better than their few fleeting kisses had promised, a potently dark sweetness that fed and stoked his hunger, the gentle softness of her mouth an aphrodisiac that punched straight into his heavy, aroused loins.

His senses consumed with a ravenous hunger he'd never felt before, Thanasis swept his hands down the curve of her back, and crushed her flush against him, holding her tight as he laid her down, the searing fusion of their mouths and tongues deepening into something primitive as he feasted on the beauty who had taunted and haunted him for so long.

Fingers dug tightly into his skull scraped lower, through the hairs of his neck and over the planes of his shoulders, and he shuddered at the sensations scorching his skin, shuddered again when her thighs parted and she wrapped her legs around him, and as he dragged his mouth over the delicate skin of her throat and felt the heavy thump of her pulse beneath his lips, he cupped a breast frustratingly covered in her tight swimsuit and felt the arousal of her hardened nipple against his palm at the same moment she circled her hips and his own arousal jutted into her pelvis.

God help him, he had never known desire could be this swift and this potent and this greedy, and he brushed his lips lower, his tongue sweeping over a collarbone that was as perfect as the rest of the body writhing beneath him…even her moans of pleasure were perfect, soaking into his ears like music, close to drowning out the voice in his head distantly shouting that he had to stop this, right now, before things went too far.

The voice cut through again, even louder.

*Stop.*

Summoning every ounce of his strength, Thanasis wrenched his mouth from the nectar of Lucie's flesh and pulled himself away from her.

The silence that followed was stark, the thumps of his weighty heart the only sound to cut through.

*Theos*, he could hardly breathe.

The sudden pleasure withdrawal of Thanasis's ravenous mouth and the glorious heat of his body left Lucie completely disoriented. Dazed, she blinked up at him, hand fluttering to her pounding heart, barely able to snatch the smallest of breaths. Her body was on fire.

There was a deep, throbbing ache between her legs as though the very core of herself had turned into lava.

Dear heavens, so that was what a real kiss felt like. Like your bones were melting into liquid.

As she watched the rapid rise and fall of Thanasis's perfect chest and the pulse throbbing in his tight jaw, her other hand absently fluttered to her mouth, fingers exploring the delicate skin his lips had just ravaged. The trail his tongue had made against her neck burned deliciously.

'That should not have happened,' he stated heavily, breaking the stunned silence.

It was like he'd tipped a bucket of ice water over her head. All the heady, joyous zings careering through her blood froze in their tracks.

He twisted back to face her with a dark, forbidding expression. 'Your feelings for me are false.'

Utterly confused, she scrambled upright and swallowed. 'How can you say that?'

There was an implacability to the way he was looking at her. Only the heaviness of his breaths betrayed the effect their moment together had had on him.

'Listen to me,' he said roughly before taking her hands and placing them flat on top of his palms. 'You feel that, yes? The touch of our hands?'

She almost wanted to deny it. It felt like Thanasis had given her a glimpse of heaven and was now denying it even existed.

'You feel it because it is true and quantifiable. Whatever else you think you feel for me, it doesn't exist because it can't—without the memories, there are no feelings because there cannot be because there is nothing for the feelings to touch on.'

'But they're there. *I* feel them,' she protested, and wrapped her fingers tightly around his hands. 'I feel them the same way I can feel your skin against mine.'

He shook his head with that same implacable assurance. 'No. You feel them because that is what you want to feel, because you feel you must for my sake, but they are not true. In time your real feelings for me will develop organically and they will be true, but you cannot force them and I will not take advantage of their absence.'

'You can't tell me I didn't feel what I just felt then,' she said, searching his eyes with something close to desperation. Could he be right? *Was* she trying to force feelings on herself? Whether he was right or wrong, all the sensations she'd just experienced in his arms... She had never, *ever* experienced anything like that before, a kiss that had made her come close to spontaneously combusting. 'Or tell me you didn't feel it too.'

God damn that Thanasis wished he could. And God damn that he wished he could just tell her the truth, and it unnerved him to know how close he'd come to telling her exactly that in the moment before she'd blown his mind with a kiss. A whisker. He'd been a whisker away from telling her the truth and blowing up his life.

He couldn't tell her the truth but nor could he let her believe that any feelings she might have for him were ghosts of her past feelings, because those feelings had never existed.

A man had his limits and Thanasis had just found his.

'Of course I felt it too.' He groaned and tugged his hands away from hers, running them furiously through his hair.

He could still feel it, the entirety of his body alive to the flame that had just incinerated them both.

'The chemistry between us has always been strong.' So strong that they'd both fought it like warriors. 'But chemistry isn't what we're talking about. All you know of your missing memories is what you've been told—you have nothing tangible to pin them to and nothing real to pin your feelings to, and until you do, I cannot in good conscience allow anything to happen between us.' He fixed her with a stare. 'I won't.'

Never. Especially not under the weight of a lie.

God damn it, why had he let that happen? He'd known it would be hard keeping Lucie at arm's length whilst playing the role of devoted fiancé but hadn't guessed it would be impossible.

A noise too much like real life cut through the tension-filled silence, and it took a long moment for Thanasis to realise it was the sound of a reprieve.

With a silent prayer to whichever deity had taken pity on him, he reached into his back pocket and pulled out his private phone. 'I must answer this.'

Getting to his feet, painfully aware of the arousal still so tight in his loins and of the unsteadiness of his legs, Thanasis crossed the bridge of his pool.

'Thanasis.'

He turned his head to the sound of Lucie's voice.

Her eyes held his for a long breath before she gave a small smile. 'Thank you.'

A cloud of emotion filled and pushed against his chest, and he closed his eyes briefly before continuing to the balustrade.

His back to her, he put the phone to his ear. *'Yassou.'*

'How is she?' Alexis asked, getting straight to the point.

It took everything he had not to turn back round to look at her.

*Theos,* he could taste her as fresh as if her sweet tongue were still dancing against his. Feel the softness of her skin beneath his fingers. The hardness of her nipple against his palm.

He swallowed to answer. 'Doing well.'

'She is with you?'

This time he couldn't resist looking even as his hackles rose at the contemptuous tone Alexis used when referring to Lucie.

*She* was still sitting on the sofa. She'd pulled her knees up to her chest. Her stare was exactly where he'd known it would be. Even with the distance between them, he could see the concentration on her face, see her thinking with the same strength as the stare boring into him.

And then her lips curved into a smile. A real smile. Lucie's Aphrodite smile. A smile she'd bestowed him with only once in their previous incarnation, on their very first meet, right before his deliberately acerbic dig about her boots.

He blew out slowly and turned away. 'Yes.'

'Any signs of her memories returning?'

'No.' He almost—almost—wished they would.

'Good. Everything is contained this end.'

'And this end.' Dangerously contained.

'The paparazzi took pictures of you two walking Piraeus harbour. Holding her hand was a nice touch.'

His hackles rose even higher. His voice gained an edge. 'I'm glad you think so.'

'I've discussed things with my father and Rebecca, and we've agreed on a million-euro payment for her silence. You will match it?'

Outrage at this speared so deeply that if Alexis Tsaliki had been standing in front of him, Thanasis's fist would have connected with his nose without a second thought.

Breathing heavily to get a grip on his temper, entirely aware that Lucie was still watching him, Thanasis lowered his voice and growled, 'Twenty million each.'

Alexis laughed.

'One million is an *insult*.'

'It will be two million if you match it, more than she would earn in her lifetime.'

'Irrelevant,' he snarled. 'Your family might think her expendable but I will not see her paid off so cheaply when, without her, we would all have lost everything by now. Twenty each or I tell her the truth this minute and leave all our fates to the gods.'

He heard a sharp suck of air.

Good. Let Alexis think he meant it. He deserved it for his contempt and the cruelty of what all the Tsalikis were doing to her.

This wasn't a game. This was Lucie's life.

Bad enough that he was playing his part in it, but this was her mother and the people she regarded as family conspiring against her without any care for what the truth would do to her.

Thanasis had no control over what the truth would do but he could play his part in making it more palatable for her to live with.

After a long silence, Alexis finally said, 'Okay. Twenty each. But you are playing a dangerous game, my friend.'

'No, I am trying to save you from losing a sister.' Hadn't he warned Rebecca that she stood to lose Lucie? Clearly she'd not taken his warning on board or shared it with the rest of her family.

'She is not my sister.'

An image flashed in Thanasis's mind. Lucie's face in that early moment in her hospital bed when he'd told her the world at large considered her a Tsaliki daughter and sister in all but blood and name. The amazement and delight in her expression.

Alexis might not regard Lucie as his sister but she thought of him as her brother.

Responding with a voice cold enough to freeze the Aegean, Thanasis said, 'And you are not my friend. Goodbye.'

He disconnected the call then had to breathe all the way into his twisted guts to stop himself hurling his phone over the balustrade.

*This* was why he'd fought tooth and nail to keep Lucie at a strict arm's length.

One kiss. One goddam kiss. It had softened him up and humanised her in the way he'd always known he must never allow, not with someone he despised with such strong passion because how could he keep his future marriage pure living with such heady, twisted temptation?

He pulled more ragged air into his lungs.

He didn't know when his feelings for Lucie had first shifted but he was starting to understand that she'd never deserved his loathing any more than she deserved Alexis's contempt.

Shifted feelings and increasing guilt or not, there was too much at stake to confess the truth before the wedding, too many lives and livelihoods at stake to walk away.

He might have thought this whole charade wrong from the start, but he'd gone along with it and would continue playing along because there was still no better option. He needed Lucie to marry him. They all needed her to marry him. Even Lucie did, and he must never let the chemistry between them win before the truth could be told.

He sensed movement behind him and turned to find her crossing the narrow bridge.

Blood filled his head, all his senses whirring back to life as she neared him. The taste of her in his mouth strengthened like a taunt.

She stopped before him like a proud goddess with her chin lifted and a hint of defiance ringing in the all-seeing eyes. 'What you just said before your phone call, about all my feelings for you being false…'

The blood in his head began to pound.

He held his breath.

'I don't believe they are,' she finished. And then she smiled her Aphrodite smile. 'But I get why it bothers you that they are and why you need me to be certain—'

'There can be no certainty until your memories come back,' he interrupted roughly. 'I could tell you anything and you have no way of knowing if it is the truth or not.'

Her Aphrodite smile didn't diminish an iota. 'You can tell me anything and I have no way of verifying it.'

'Exactly.' Now, at last, she was getting it. Thanasis might not be able to tell her the truth but he could damn well open her mind to the possibility that everything she'd been told about her missing memories could all be lies. Open her mind so when he revealed the truth on their wedding night, the shock would be absorbed.

'But if you keep putting me at arm's length, how am I ever going to get to know the real you and know if my feelings are true or not?' she said, a glint of stubborn knowing in her eyes. 'Because, let's face it, my memories might never come back.'

Lucie laughed to see the frustration flash on Thanasis's gorgeous face.

Once she'd got over her shock at his declaration that the most thrilling moment of her life was something that should never have happened, she'd realised nothing had changed and that he was still trying to protect her from both himself and herself.

Well, no more. She'd spent days trying to be compliant and behaving in a way she'd been told was for the best because of her head wound, and now it was time to take back control and narrate her own story rather than let others dictate it for her, and that included Adonis's sexier replacement.

Reaching for Thanasis's hand, marvelling at the power contained in it, she pulled it to her mouth and rubbed his fingers against her lips. 'See?' she said, gleefully gazing into a stare she could see fighting to put the shutters back down. 'Whatever my memory issues, I still have free will, and I had free will when I kissed you, just as you had free will when you kissed me back and free will when you pulled away. We both know I will marry you whatever happens, so stop treating me with kid gloves. I promise you, I'm unbreakable.'

Jaw clenched tightly, he pulled his hand away. 'No one is unbreakable.'

'I made it through my childhood in one piece and with a hide built of rhino skin. Trust me, there is nothing you or anyone can do to hurt me on anything more than a superficial level, so gloves off and mask off—I want to know the real Thanasis Antoniadis and make up my own mind about the man he is and let my feelings develop in the organic way he suggested just twenty minutes ago.'

That had him, she thought with yet more glee that *might* be an effect of the giddiness of his kisses still streaming in her veins or *might* be due to finally snookering him with his own words.

Not allowing him time to interject, Lucie pointed in the distance to where the early morning sun was rising in an arc between the V created by two mountains directly in their line of vision. It was as if a straight line had been created from balcony to V, sweeping over the roof of the chapel for good measure. 'First question. Is it coincidence that this section of balcony is completely aligned with the rising sun?' She laughed at his disbelieving expression. 'I want to know *you*, Thanasis. Everything about you. So get talking.'

Sometimes, Thanasis thought, a man had to know when he was beaten, and there was no doubt in his mind that on this occasion Lucie had outplayed him with nothing more than a twisting of his words.

The quick brain that never missed a trick was back in full functioning order, but this wasn't the confrontational Lucie he'd spent two months despising. This was a different Lucie. This was the Lucie he'd spent all those long weeks determined not to know.

He hadn't wanted to know her.

For all that she'd given as good as she'd got, *he'd* been the instigator of the war that had erupted between them. It had all been him.

But that was then and now everything had changed.

He could do nothing to change what had already passed but he could play along and give Lucie the chance his determination to hate her had meant he'd refused to give her before. Get to know the real Lucie Burton and not the warped picture he'd pre-painted in his head, a painting made with all the wrong colours and strokes. Now it was time to allow her real colours to shine through.

As painful as it was to admit, he owed her that much.

His mind set, he filled his lungs with clean Sephone

air and met the expectant, sparkling black eyes. 'Even though you have presented me with a closed question, I will enter the spirit of the game as the game was intended and give a full answer.'

She gave a full wattage beam.

'The villa was designed with the rise and fall of the sun in mind. You have to get up early to see it, but when the sun first rises, the only light on the island comes from between those two mountains.'

'So my balcony and the balcony on the other side of your room must face west, then?'

He nodded. 'When the sun sets, our vantage point gives the illusion that it is melting into the sea.'

'Okay, but whose idea was it to capture both the sunrise and sunset in the villa's design? Yours or Thomas's?'

'Mine.'

'Now we're talking.'

He narrowed his eyes in question.

She rose onto her tiptoes and tapped the end of his nose. 'It means that you appreciate the wonders of the world.'

His chest filling at the teasing but affectionate gesture, Thanasis took a step back.

While he was willing to play along with Lucie's wish to get to know him better, and knew it was only fair that he should get to know the real Lucie better too, he could not in all good conscience allow himself to play along with the role of her lover. Not now. Not with the taste of her still alive on his tongue and the heavy weight of desire still so thick in his loins. It had taken more strength than he'd known he possessed to pull away from her, and he couldn't be certain he would find that same strength again, not when she was so warm and passionate and willing and…

He snatched a breath.

He needed to keep Lucie at a physical arm's length until they married. Just a few more days, that was all, and then the truth would be revealed.

It was even possible that she would forgive him.

'I can't say anyone has said that to me before,' he murmured.

'You must hide that part of your nature really well. Weren't you tempted to build your villa up there?' She indicated the slightly higher of the two mountains.

'That is where I originally wanted the villa built, yes. The only thing that stopped me was the terrain—it would have been too dangerous for the building crew. There is a particular spot up there where you can watch the sun rise and set. It is the only vantage point on the whole island better than what we have here.'

'Will you take me there?'

'When you are better.'

She pulled an unimpressed face.

'The golf buggies can't reach it so you have to walk, and it's a long, often steep walk,' he explained. 'Give yourself a few days to fully rebuild your strength.'

She eyed him for a moment and then grinned. 'Okay. But only if you get Elias to make me more of those delicious keftedes for me to build my strength with.'

He couldn't stop himself from grinning back. 'You have a deal.'

But a deal he absolutely would not seal with a kiss.

# CHAPTER EIGHT

THE CHAPEL WAS much bigger than Lucie had anticipated from her vantage point on Thanasis's balcony, but it was too hot to goggle at it from the outside and she practically threw herself through the arched door.

It was every bit as cool inside as she'd hoped.

'Better?' the hulk who'd entered the chapel with slightly more decorum asked drily.

On this, Lucie's second full day in Sephone, she'd woken early again and had swum round to Thanasis's east-facing balcony. He'd been waiting for her by the pool steps.

She'd grinned up at him. After all, he hadn't actually made her give the promise not to swim unsupervised again.

He'd shaken his head in mock disappointment and handed her a towel to dry herself. And then they'd sat on his balcony sofa and watched the sun rise together over coffee and *bougatsa* as if it had all been pre-planned.

'Much.' She fanned herself with the back of her hand to rid her face of the last of the perspiration that had broken out on it during the short buggy ride from the villa.

'I spent every summer in Greece during my schooldays. You'd think I'd remember how hot it gets here.'

'When was your last summer spent here?'

'When I was eighteen. Full time work unfortunately does not allow for long, lazy summers.' Or didn't. She didn't have a job any more. Of all the things she'd given up to marry Thanasis and save their two families, her career was the only one she felt real pangs of regret over. Of all the memories lost, her resignation was the one she didn't want to come back. She had a feeling it would be a scene too distressing to want to relive. In her six years there, the Kelly Holden Design team had come to feel like family. It was a family she'd gate-crashed her way into but still a family. Or a version of one.

No point harking back to something that was already done, she told herself resolutely, and craned her head around at the vast space with its high, ornate pillars and frescoed ceiling in which she and Thanasis would soon marry. It really was the most incredible and awe-inspiring of spaces, like someone had Greek-ified the Duomo, shrunk it to vaguely manageable proportions, and transported it to Sephone.

A thought struck her and she whipped her stare to Thanasis. 'How can this be here if the island was abandoned millennia ago? I didn't think they had chapels back then?'

'I had it built alongside the villa.'

'Wow. So it's less than ten years old? It could have been standing for centuries.'

'That was the feel I was aspiring to.'

'You're religious?'

'Not particularly. It was for my mother. Church is a regular feature of her life. She always suffers guilt if she misses Sunday mass.'

'I think that has to be the most thoughtful gift I've ever heard of,' she said, astounded.

'She's my mother,' he said matter-of-factly before pulling a musing face. 'And it has come in handy for our purposes.'

'There is that,' she agreed. 'Did you imagine you would marry in here when you built it? Or did it just work out that way when we settled on marrying on the island?'

He took a while to answer, and when he spoke, his words were slow. 'When I saw it completed I knew it would be where I marry.'

'Bet you never imagined it would be with me,' she jested, and was rewarded with a short, non-committal laugh. 'So who's marrying us? Do you have a permanent priest here?'

'No. There is a semi-retired priest in Kos who travels over whenever my mother's here. He will be officiating.'

'I assume the ceremony will be conducted in Greek?'

'You assume correctly.'

'Good.'

He raised an eyebrow.

'It's fitting,' she said. 'It would be sacrilegious to have the service in English. This chapel, this whole island, it's Greek to its core… What time are we actually marrying?'

'Six p.m.'

'Is that to escape the worst of the heat?'

'Partly, but mostly because when the service is finished we will have the photos taken on the stretch of beach where the sun sets.'

'So we'll have the sunset as our background?'

'Precisely.'

'Sounds perfect and extremely romantic. The media will lap it up.'

He grimaced. 'That was the idea behind it.'

'Don't worry,' she assured him. 'First and foremost, this marriage is for business purposes and there's no point pretending otherwise. That anything else has come out of it is just sheer good luck—let's face it, it could have gone completely the other way. Can you imagine how awful it would have been if we'd hated each other?' She imagined it would have been unbearable. Lucie always felt awkward and prickly when in the company of people who disliked her. Whenever Athena had gone through her spates of being mean to her, Lucie had always coiled into herself and grown defensive spikes. Thank God Thanasis had been prepared to give her a chance and not park her in the camp of being his enemy.

But his family hadn't been prepared to do that. Strange how this hadn't bothered her when she'd first guessed it but now, just a day later, it made her chest tighten. She supposed it was the fact of their wedding no longer being an abstract thing. She was here, in the thick of all the preparations and glued to the side of the man who would soon be her husband… Well, glued as much as he would allow.

There had definitely been a shift for the better in the way Thanasis was around her. There was a greater sense of looseness about him, not just in his frame but in his speech, less of a sense that he was weighing each word carefully before allowing himself to speak, more gesticulation and more glimpses of the good-humoured man she'd dined with her first night on the island. She was growing to like a lot about him. She liked his patience, of course…that had already been established. Liked that he was happy to play Getting to Know You for hours even though he must already know so much about her and had probably relayed many of the stories she'd coaxed out of him before. Small, mostly insignificant stories that built a picture of a man from the loving, stable background she'd once longed for. A man for whom family was everything, and she had the strong sense that once this controlled bear of a man loved you, there would be nothing he would not do for you and nothing he would not do to protect you, and Lucie supposed it was a sign of his love for her that he was trying to protect her from herself.

Because what she didn't like was the physical distance he'd imposed between them. Even the small signs of affection had gone. If she stood or sat too close to him, he'd visibly stiffen and edge away. When she'd covered his hand over lunch he'd gently but firmly moved it away. When their ankles had brushed under the dining table he'd adjusted his position so his long legs were aimed in a different direction.

His control was impressive and infuriating because that heady, passionate kiss had unleashed something in her, an ache she carried everywhere, in every cell of her body. There was not a minute spent in his company when Lucie didn't long for him to just touch her, a longing made worse knowing it had unleashed something in him too. She could feel it like a vibration, the tempered desire beating beneath the powerful body, and she could see it too, a dark pulse in his eyes before he snapped it away with a blink.

She knew he'd imposed this physical distance for her sake, and while she appreciated his reasonings, she would look around his glorious garden and the romantic fairy tale it was being transformed into for their wedding day, and experience that thrilling rush of emotions, and it all felt so *real*. Her and Thanasis. And if they were real then it meant the fact that his family hated her was real too.

Another family she didn't fit in with.

She would make them like her, she decided resolutely. Well, try. After all, she'd had nothing to do with the war between the two families. In reality, only Georgios and Petros had. Everyone else was just a bystander. Collateral damage.

'What are you thinking about?' Thanasis asked, cutting through her ruminations.

'Everything.' She laughed and shook her head, wishing she could wrap her arms around him and breathe in his gorgeous scent. Wishing, if she did that, he would wrap his arms around her and not stiffen and then politely extract himself from her hold.

'I was thinking about your cynicism about our two families ever truly burying the hatchet. I think it could happen.'

'Our families have been at war for decades,' he reminded her. 'Too much has happened for it to be forgotten. The bad feelings run too deep.'

'I know, but if you and I were able to see past all that and build something together...' She lifted her shoulders. 'There has to be hope the rest of our families can build bridges too, because otherwise what's the point?'

'The point is saving our respective businesses and fortunes.'

'If that's the case, if the hatchet isn't actually buried, what's to stop your father or Georgios picking it up and burying it into each other's backs again once the businesses are saved?' Saying this, Lucie knew not even a written guarantee would stop Georgios from going after his nemesis again if the mood struck him.

How the big-hearted man with an even bigger smile could be so vengeful was beyond her understanding, and that there were two elderly Greek men out there who'd been unable to take a hard look at themselves in the mirror and say a firm *no* when the 'pranks' they'd played on each other had turned so dangerous just blew her mind.

'They know what's at stake if they do,' he assured her.

'But there has to be more than that to stop them starting it all up again. Sure, with you and Alexis now in charge there's not going to be the blatant sabotage of each other's fleets—and I know I've probably said it before, but I was horrified when I learned Georgios was behind the fuel replacement in your ocean liners that destroyed all those engines. I love him dearly but that was a terrible thing to do—but what's to stop them making it even more personal if they hate each other so much?'

And how would that affect *them*? she suddenly thought with what could only be described as panic. Would things escalate to the extent she would be forced to choose between her new family and her stepfamily?

She might never have felt like a true Tsaliki but they'd all been good to her. Georgios had doted on her as if she were one of his own. The boys, all older except her half-brother, Loukas, had teased and looked out for her in the same way they'd teased and looked out for Athena. As for Athena, with her being only two years older than Lucie and the only girl in a household of boys, it was natural that they should have gravitated together. Sure, Athena could be a Grade A bitch and there were times Lucie would prefer to bury herself alive than be in her company, but when she was on form she was brilliant. When you knew and loved someone as much as Lucie knew and loved Athena, you forgave the less palatable sides of their nature.

How was she supposed to choose between all that and her new family who didn't even like her? They hated her!

'My father has given me his word, and Alexis has given his word to keep Georgios in line,' Thanasis told her steadily.

She pulled a sceptical face and tried her hardest to swallow back the growing angst.

He folded his arms across the gloriously broad chest she ached to bury her face in, and rested his back against a marble pillar. 'Trust me, *matia mou*. They both know how close they have come to losing everything. The hatchet might not be buried but, I promise you, the war is over.'

Loving and hating his endearment—loving how tender it sounded on his tongue but hating that it was the closest thing to affection he would currently allow between them—she expelled the last of her sudden panic with a sigh. 'I'm sorry. I forgot for a minute that you and Alexis put all the hard work in and dotted all the I's and crossed all the T's months ago. There would have been no point in you and I agreeing to marry in the first place if we didn't have those assurances from them.'

*'Akrivos,'* he said. Exactly.

But now the mentions of her stepbrother had stirred something else in her brain. 'Were Alexis and Athena really the only members of my family you had contact with before my accident?'

'In a face-to-face capacity, yes. Why do you ask?'

'I don't know.' And she didn't, not really, more that her brain was trying to take hold of something in her memory bank, the whisper of a recent conversation… with her mother? It had to be. Who else had she spoken to that she cared for since being hospitalised other than Thanasis and her mother? She had no phone so hadn't been able to make any calls since arriving on Sephone, and it occurred to her that she'd not given a single thought since her arrival of Thanasis's offer to have a replacement phone flown over for her.

To her surprise, she found she didn't want a replacement. Not yet. There was something quite freeing about being uncontactable here on this island paradise, and besides, everyone she loved and cared for would be part of the five hundred strong party that would be descending on Sephone in a few days' time for the wedding.

For the first time since their kiss, Thanasis's stare captured hers with the intensity of old. 'Do you have a memory coming back?'

Returning to the whispers in her memory bank, Lucie shook her head in frustration. 'I don't think so. Whatever I'm searching for is recent but I think the drugs I was fed in hospital have blurred things for me.' She shook her head again and tried to be philosophical about it. She had two months of her life missing and was fixating on one little nebulous thing? Sometimes she really needed to give her head a good wobble. 'Oh, well, what's another lost memory between friends...? Does that sound like a helicopter to you?'

She was quite sure she could hear a rotor.

Thanasis, his watchful eyes still on her, craned his ear and nodded. 'That must be your wedding dress.'

'Clever dress to fly a helicopter,' she deadpanned, and was rewarded with a loosening of his features and that glorious spark that always zinged between them whenever he hopped onto her wavelength.

Wryly, he said, 'For the amount it's costing, I'm hoping it can cook steak too.'

Almost giddy to have shaken off the disquiet that had sneaked up on her out of nowhere, she had to practically glue her feet to the intricately patterned cool flooring to stop herself from reaching for him. 'I guess that means it'll soon be dress-fitting time… What kind of dress is it?' Funny, she hadn't thought to ask that before.

'A wedding dress.'

'Very helpful. I meant what *kind* of wedding dress.'

'I do not have the faintest idea.' Pointedly, he added, 'I would assume it's white but if your wardrobe is anything to go by, it might very well be black.'

She curtsied in her short, black, strapless playsuit and flat black sandals.

He laughed loudly, the deep sound bouncing off the chapel's walls, a glorious sound that didn't just soak into her ears but soaked into her skin and veins, feeding the longing for him it felt like she'd been carrying for ever, and meeting his eyes, the lines around them creased with his amusement, she could do nothing to stop the sigh of her longing from seeping out…

His eyes flickered at the sound and in an instant the laughter died. The lines uncreased and the light on his face dimmed.

The air enveloping them thickened and suddenly the chapel was filled with a silence more complete than anything Lucie had ever known. For one long, breathless moment, anticipation that he was going to unfold himself from his prop against the pillar and haul her into his arms held her hostage.

She didn't know if she wanted to cry or scream when she watched the shutters of his eyes come down with one forceful blink, and when he unfolded himself from his prop against the pillar, it was with his usual languidness.

'We should probably meet the design team so you can

have your dress fitting, so shall we?' He indicated the door as if nothing had just passed between them.

Lucie summoned a smile. Or something she hoped resembled a smile. 'Sure, let's go and fight our way through the furnace just so I can be used as a human pin cushion.'

The lines around his eyes creased a touch. 'I'm sure that if you keep still and let the team do their job, Francois will be careful not to let them stab you too many times.'

'A cheering thought, and as a reward for the patience I'm going to have to display whilst being used as a pin cushion, you can take me up into the mountains later to watch the sunset.'

Not giving him the chance to argue with her, Lucie sauntered out of the chapel and into the oven that was the great outdoors. It actually felt quite cooling compared to the furnace inside her.

To Lucie's disappointment, she spent so long being used as a human mannequin that by the time she was released from the purgatory of the dress-fitting room, the sun was already starting to set. That wasn't to say it had been a nightmare—her dress was gorgeous and entirely in a style she adored, which was to be expected seeing as she'd had a say in its design even if she didn't remember having that say, and Francois and his team had all treated her as if she were a princess. As an added bonus, she hadn't been stabbed once—it was just that trying to hold a conversation for three hours when all she could see and think of was the expression in Thanasis's eyes before he'd pulled the shutters back down had been close to impossible. He was driving her crazy!

He continued to drive her crazy with his body language that night over dinner, all pulsing looks when she caught him unguarded combined with utter physical control of himself. They exchanged not so much as a touch of a finger between them. It was a torture that continued the next day, from the moment she swam to his balcony for breakfast right until the time came for them to head into the mountains to watch the sunset.

Changing, at Thanasis's insistence, out of the sparkly black flip flops he'd decreed unsuitable for trekking in, Lucie shoved her feet into her only vaguely suitable footwear, her chunky black calf-length boots, and met him at the front of the villa. He was in the driving seat of the golf buggy they would use to take them as far and as high as they could go before they had to walk. In the back seat, an enormous backpack filled with food for their adventure.

His gaze flicked to her as she stepped out of the door, then dropped to her feet. There was a long moment of stillness, as if someone had accidentally pressed pause on him, and Lucie had a sudden certainty that came from nowhere that he was going to comment with, 'Nice boots,' before he blinked himself back to life and welcomed her with a smile instead of words.

She walked over and showed him the tube of sunscreen in her hand. 'Can you put some on my back for me please? I can't reach.'

She watched his reaction, noted the tightening of his

smile and the subtle flicker in his eyes, and knew applying sunscreen to her flesh was the very last thing he wanted to do.

She almost laughed.

It was the first time she'd needed to ask him. Daylight hours on Sephone had been spent avoiding the scorching heat of the sun but the climb they were going to embark on would leave her exposed.

*Bad luck, Thanasis. Got you with this one, haven't I?*

With a sharp nod, he held his hand out for the tube.

She passed it to him. For the first time since their legs had brushed two nights ago, skin met skin as the pads of their fingers touched. But it was no lingering touch. Thanasis practically snatched his hand away before climbing out of the buggy.

Turning her back to him, she lifted her hair with one hand and held her breath.

Thanasis gritted his teeth, squeezed some of the lotion onto his hand, and told himself to grow a pair. It was human skin, nothing more. So what if it happened to be Lucie's skin? There wasn't all that much flesh that needed to be covered, mostly the shoulders and down to the base of her shoulder blades. Her black vest with its thin straps covered the rest of it…the thin straps she lifted her free hand to tug down her shoulders so he could apply the lotion unimpeded, confirming what he'd spent the day determined not to notice. That Lucie wasn't wearing a bra.

He took a deep breath to clear his suddenly constricted throat and put his hands to the top of her back.

With brisk, wide strokes, he rubbed the lotion into the silken skin, fingers sliding over the nape of her neck, over the slender shoulders, and lower down until every centimetre of exposed flesh was protected.

He would never know what compelled his fingers to trace up her spine or why her shiver compelled his mouth to drop a kiss to her ear.

Breathing heavily, he stepped away from her and forced his thrumming body back into the buggy.

# CHAPTER NINE

THE DRIVE TO the mountain and to the point where the buggy could go no further took only twenty minutes. They were twenty of the longest minutes of Lucie's life, and when Thanasis pulled the buggy to a stop in a natural clearing, her heart was still beating erratically.

Asking him to put the sunscreen on her had been necessary, but also a fun way to needle the man who'd developed a rigid determination to keep his hands to himself. She hadn't anticipated that the dial of her longing for him, carried in every fibre of her being, would turn even higher. From the tension vibrating from the powerful frame sitting so closely beside her, and the clipped way he spoke when describing features of the mountain they were about to climb and talking about the natural fauna they were driving through, Thanasis for once being the one to drive the conversation, it was a suffering that was shared.

She could still feel his lips on her ear.

First removing two bottles of water, one of which he passed to her, he shrugged the huge backpack onto his back with the same ease Lucie slung a handbag over a shoulder. 'Ready?'

Lucie looked up. The natural trail Thanasis was going to lead her on to the top of the mountain didn't look too difficult to manage, at least not yet. The high trees surrounding them looked as if they would provide welcome shade from a sun still blazing its rays on the island. If they kept a steady pace, they'd reach the summit within the hour.

Feeling more able to breathe properly now she wasn't trapped on the buggy with his giant body so close to hers and his body language telling her loud and clear not to even think of breaching the tiny distance between them, she looked back at him and nodded.

'Then let's go. Stay close.'

She snorted. 'That's the last thing you want me to do.'

He fixed her with a stare. 'No, the last thing I want you to do is fall and hurt yourself. Or get bitten by a snake.'

'There's snakes?'

'If snakes frighten you, tell me now and we will go back to the villa.'

The last of the tight angst she'd been carrying inside her melted away. She grinned. 'You're not getting out of this that easily. I'm not scared of snakes, I was just surprised when you mentioned them. I've never seen a snake in all my years visiting Greece.'

'Snakes tend to avoid Athens and I can't see them sneaking onto your stepfather's yacht,' he commented drily. 'Here, in the mountains, it is different. Tread carefully, especially in non-shaded areas—they like to sunbathe.'

'Lazy so-and-sos.'

To her delight and relief, Thanasis's tight features relaxed into amusement and with a spring of happiness in her step, she set off beside him.

'Do you do much hiking?' she asked as they started up a shaded, gentle incline.

'I used to. Not so much now.'

'What kind of answer is that?'

He cast her with a swift glance. 'Are we playing your game again?'

'Too right. So proper answers, thank you.'

'When I was at university a group of us would go camping at weekends and holidays and find new places to explore.'

'You, camping?' Much as she tried, she could not imagine Thanasis squeezed inside a tent.

He laughed. 'I cannot say I enjoyed that aspect quite so much, but the camaraderie and adventure made it worth it.'

'And the beer?' she guessed.

'That was part of it,' he agreed. 'We still try to meet up a few times a year but I've not been able to join the others for the last two trips. I missed a week hiking in South California earlier this year.'

'All the stuff with the business?'

'Yes. It has taken every minute of my time.'

'Well, hopefully our marriage will go a long way to

putting all your business troubles behind you, and you can start living your life properly again.'

'That is mine and everyone else's hope, and when we are all able to start living properly again, Antoniadis and Tsaliki, it will all be thanks to you.'

'You know me, here to help,' she jested.

He came to a sudden stop. 'No, *matia mou*, do not try to downplay what you are doing. If not for your agreement to marry me, both businesses would be lucky to still be clinging on. Your selflessness has ensured our survival.'

'Hardly selfless, and you agreed to it too.'

'I agreed because it was the only hope we had of clawing our way out of the mess. You agreed knowing you would gain nothing from it.'

'Other than my stepfamily's survival,' she pointed out.

'That is my point. You entered into our agreement for everyone else's sake when you didn't owe anybody anything.'

'Apart from a lifetime of being loved by them, that's absolutely spot on.'

Thanasis had to bite his tongue and swallow back his anger. If there was any love on the Tsalikis' part for Lucie, they had a strange way of showing it.

They set off again. 'How did your stepsiblings get on with your mother when you were growing up?'

He knew his question had him skirting dangerous territory but that was a risk he was willing to take. Lucie needed to be prepared in some small way for what was coming when the truth came out.

'They all got on fine. They'd had so many stepmums by the time she came along that I imagine they took her presence in their stride. She never tried to mother them so that probably helped. Saying that,' she added with a cackle of laughter, 'she never much tried to mother me, either.'

Another bite of the tongue and the swallow back of anger.

Thanasis had never imagined he could despise someone more than Georgios Tsaliki but his fourth wife roused a different, colder kind of loathing in him, and he had to bite his tongue another time to stop himself from pointing out that Athena and Stelios had never had another stepmother before Rebecca Tsaliki usurped their own mother.

They'd reached a steep incline that required concentration to navigate despite the rope he'd had put along its edge for support, and they didn't speak as they made their way up it. To reach the top of the incline you had to climb a sheer drop that was only six foot and which Thanasis could manage easily, but when you didn't quite reach five foot it meant you needed help.

'I will lift you,' he said with an impassiveness only his racing pulses would prove was a lie.

He shrugged off the backpack then stood behind her. 'Ready?'

'Yep.'

He put his hands securely to her waist and lifted her until her bottom, clad only in a pair of black denim shorts, was face high to him and Lucie was waist high to the ledge and able to swing herself over. The last he saw of her was the black boots that had earlier given him a cold case of *déjà vu* before her face peered over the edge and she grinned down at him. 'You coming up?'

Lucie thought she might just have discovered heaven on earth.

The top of the mountain was ruggedly sparse of vegetation but the thickness of the picnic blanket Thanasis had spread out stopped the rocks and prickly plants beneath them from jabbing into their skin and allowed her to do nothing but marvel at the scene unfolding before her. Oh, and eat the delicious spread of food Elias and his assistant had whipped up for them, of which she'd stuffed as much as she could manage into her belly. Stretched out on his back beside her, propping himself up on his elbows having eaten his fill too and playing the most major part in the heavenly scene, Thanasis.

'Thank you for bringing me here.' She turned her stare to him with a smile. She had never in her life seen such a spectacular vista, similar to the view from their balconies but so much, much more. The setting sun was not yet low enough to melt into the sea but its reflection had turned the Aegean's horizon a golden orange, the distant islands darkening and becoming all the more striking for it.

The man who outshone the vista in the beauty stakes responded with a smile that crinkled the lines around his eyes. *'Parakalo.'* After a beat, he added, 'I brought my sister here once. She spent more time complaining about the patchy phone signal than admiring the beauty nature has to offer.'

'I guess the world would be very boring if we all liked the same things.'

'I don't think Lydia and I have ever agreed on anything that we both like,' he commented drily. 'If she didn't have so much of both our parents in her, I would believe she was adopted.'

She laughed and studied the piece of pottery Thanasis had found when they'd reached the summit and he'd been deciding the perfect place to lay the blanket. Faded black paint with what could possibly be the tip of a pair of wings painted in faded gold on it, the relic measured roughly ten inches by five inches. Its concave shape suggested it had once been a pot and Thanasis's casual dating of it as 'probably being two, three thousand years old' would have blown her mind if she had any mind left to blow. With the benefit of hindsight, Lucie realised learning she was engaged to Thanasis Antoniadis had been peak blowing of her mind. Everything else would always be lesser in comparison.

She had yet to reach peak awe over his devastating good looks though, and she carefully laid the piece of pottery down and stretched herself onto her back beside him. Wriggling her bare toes—they'd both removed their footwear—she gave a contented sigh. Her feet were a bit sore from the trek and there were a few cuts on her thighs from where spiky plants had decided to scratch her, but she didn't care in the slightest. She thought this might just be the happiest she'd ever been.

'Are you okay?' he murmured, resting his head on the blanket next to hers.

She sighed again and turned her face to the glory of his. 'I'm just perfect.'

An assessment Thanasis found himself struggling to disagree with, although she hadn't meant it in the way his brain was interpreting it.

He didn't know if it was Lucie's goddess powers coming to the fore again and giving her the ability to read minds, but when she broke the comfortable silence by saying, 'What do you like about me?' he came close to laughing.

It was a laughter that would have died before it had formed for she rolled onto her side and tucked an arm under her head to cushion it, her face so close he could see the flecks of gold dancing in the black eyes now glued to his. Any comfort at being with her vanished as the awareness he'd been controlling with sheer brute force snaked its way back through his veins.

'Getting to Know You time again,' she said with a soft, spellbinding smile, 'so full and honest answers.'

Turning his stare to the darkening clear sky, Thanasis hooked an arm above his head but, such was the force of the spell she was casting on him, couldn't bring himself to move any further away from her. 'You want to know what I like about you?' he clarified carefully.

'I want to know what it was that turned your feelings for me from what I'm guessing is resignation at the situation we'd found ourselves in, into something more.'

'I don't know. It just happened.' He couldn't stop a quick turn of his face to her. 'Like magic.'

'I can believe that.' She lifted her chin onto her forearm and inched a little closer. Her smile had a dreamy quality to it. 'But there must be something specific you like about me. I mean, I really like catching your flashes of humour, and I really like that you love your mum enough to build a chapel for her, and love your family enough to build multiple swimming pools when you never swim, and I like that when you talk about your sister, you sound both proud and indulgent, like she's someone you really love and respect even if you don't particularly understand her.'

Thanasis only realised his quick turn of face towards her had become a full-blown roll of his body when he released the curl he'd taken hold of and pulled straight without any awareness of doing so. It pinged straight back into its original ringlet form in the same way his lust for Lucie could only be suppressed into a form of stasis until one look or word or inhalation sprang it back into its natural state.

'There are many things I like about you,' he said quietly, capturing another curl. 'I like your hair and the way the curls never look the same from one day to the next. I like the way you smile with your whole face. I like your addiction to cheese and I like that you treat all the food you eat with reverence. I like the way you stand up for yourself. I like your independence of thought and I like the way you always try to take other viewpoints on board. I like that I can bring you to a view like this and know you will appreciate it as much as I do.'

It came as a shock to realise that there was nothing about Lucie that he didn't like.

Nothing at all.

Lucie found she could no longer breathe. Her heart was thumping loudly in her ears.

The green eyes gazing at her were staring as if seeing her face for the very first time.

Silence more complete than any she'd ever known had enveloped them, the air charged with an electricity she felt in every cell of her body.

A trembling finger traced a line over her shoulder and down her arm, heated vibrations from the powerful body so close to hers the tips of her breasts were brushing against his chest, buzzing deep into her skin.

His breath swirled against her mouth and the ache she'd carried for days between her legs, so subtle she'd been barely conscious of it, throbbed like a pulse of fire.

Fingers wrapped tightly around her wrists and then the heat of his breath became the heat of his mouth, an unmoving, lingering, barely controlled fusion that ended with a deep groan and one hard sweep of his tongue into her mouth before he rolled onto his back and expelled a breath so long and so hard he could have been breathing out for her too.

Hoarsely, he said, 'You cannot know how badly I want you, but, Lucie, we can't.'

Frustration came close to making her scream. Lifting herself onto her elbow, her heart smashing so hard against her ribs it was as if it were trying to escape and cling to him, she pressed her hand to his cheek. 'Why not?'

Snatching hold of her hand, he inhaled as if breathing in for them both too, his green stare as intense as she'd ever seen it. 'You know why not. Believe me, I would give anything to make love to you but...'

He cut himself off with an oath and hoisted himself up, bowing his head and dragging his fingers through his hair with the same fury she'd witnessed before.

She couldn't just see the torture he was putting himself through, but feel it too, as deeply as she felt her own torture, and when she placed a hand to his back, could feel the heavy thuds of his heart. 'What if my memories never come back? We're getting married in three days, Thanasis. Are you really suggesting we could spend a whole life together in separate beds?'

'No.'

'Then what?'

He tilted his head and slowly rolled his neck. When he finally spoke, his voice was more moderate. 'We wait until the wedding. If on our wedding night you still want to make love to me, then, believe me, you will never find a more willing groom.'

Only the finality in his tone stopped her arguing further.

It was when Lucie was climbing into bed much later that night that her first concrete memory came back. It wasn't much, just a whisper, but it was something solid. Being in Thanasis's apartment. His back had had that rigidness to it that she recognised from her time in hospital and when she'd first been discharged.

They'd been arguing, although what the argument had been about remained a mystery, but he'd walked out of the living room without a backward glance at her.

It was the same room that had been in her dream when Athena had spoken so cruelly to her.

'Hi, Gracie, how are things?' Lucie asked the youngest of her two English half-sisters the next morning, and was rewarded with a grunt that might have been *Good, thank you*, but was probably just a grunt.

In seconds, her stepmother had taken the phone from her. Charlie, Vanessa said in reference to Lucie's father, was in the shower and would call her back if he had time before he left for work. After assuring Lucie that everything was all set for them to join her for the wedding, and that it was something they were all very much looking forward to, Vanessa disconnected the call. She must have forgotten to ask how Lucie's head injury was, so her pre-prepared airy, 'I'm absolutely fine' was entirely wasted.

'Your father is busy?' Thanasis guessed shrewdly.

'I knew he would be,' she admitted. 'It is a work day and he has his routine to keep.' Her father thrived on routine and order. Which was probably why he'd always found Lucie so trying. She dredged a bright smile so as not to show her dejection. 'I would call my mum but she's probably asleep in her coffin.'

He laughed and stretched his long legs out. 'She

didn't sleep in her coffin when she was watching over you in hospital.'

'Yeah, but I bet she got them to feed the donated blood to her.'

'She did disappear a number of times.'

'See, told you.' She passed his phone back and tried not to show her fresh dejection when he took care not to let their fingers touch.

They were eating breakfast on the balcony again, enjoying a few moments of peace. The wedding was only two days away now, and activity levels on the island had gone through the roof, the workers busy setting things up through the night so that any outdoor work could be avoided in the scorching heat of the day.

There was nothing enjoyable about this torture for Lucie that early morning. She'd slept badly, oscillating between sexual frustration, something she had never suffered from before in her life, and trying to force more memories, trying to at least expand the one concrete memory that had come to her.

'Are you okay?' he asked. 'You don't seem yourself.'

She shrugged and kept her moody gaze on the rising sun. If he could read her so well that he could see through her fake bright smiles, then he'd probably hear any lie in her voice.

Lucie had assumed she would tell Thanasis about the memory that had come back to her, but now found something holding her back.

Why couldn't her first real memory of those missing months have been a good one? Why couldn't it have been of them laughing or, even better, making love, not of the aftermath of an argument where he'd walked out on her and she'd been fighting back tears she would never let him see.

*Why* wouldn't she have wanted him to see her cry? She'd never been much of a crier but she'd never been ashamed of her tears the few times they'd leaked out over her life.

And why was she too frightened to ask him about it?

But she needed to say something. 'When we were living in your apartment... Did Athena visit much?'

There was only the slightest hesitation. 'A few times that I know of. What makes you ask?'

'A dream I had.' That much she could tell him, and now she did look at him.

He'd raised an eyebrow in question.

'The other night,' she explained. 'I thought it was a dream but now I think it might have been a memory.'

'And you think that because?'

She kept her stare on him, wanting to gauge his re-action although she didn't quite know why she wanted to gauge it. 'Do you have black leather sofas and a glass coffee table?'

His face moved a little closer to hers. There was the slightest flicker in his eye. 'You remember them?'

'Yes.'

'Anything else?'

She chose her words carefully. 'Nothing specific, but in my dream Athena was laughing at me, which is nothing unusual for her but the way it made me feel in the dream was unusual. Normally whatever she says to me rolls off—the only way to deal with her is to be Teflon coated—but whatever she said had really upset me.'

There was a tightness in his voice. 'Can you remember what she said? What she was laughing about?'

'No. Is it real, then, the dream? Did I discuss it with you?'

'No, but, Lucie...' His features loosened a touch. Slowly, he reached for her. Suddenly she found herself holding her breath as his thumb traced over her cheek. 'Athena has always been poisonous to you. She *is* poison. If you remember nothing else, remember that.'

The small, tender act of intimacy was over before she could take a breath. Before she could even open her mouth to speak, he expelled a short decisive breath and, with a rueful smile, got to his feet. 'I need to get changed. My helicopter will be landing shortly.'

She stared at him dumbly. 'You're going somewhere?'

'I have business in Athens.'

She stared even more dumbly. This was the first she'd heard of it. 'Can I come?'

'I'm afraid not.'

'Why not?'

'Because it's business and I need you here to supervise the wedding preparations.'

'That's what Griselda's paid to do.'

'We are marrying in two days, *matia mou*. One of us needs to be here, to be on hand if anything important crops up. You might be needed for another dress fitting too.'

Then, as if her morning for shocks wasn't already complete, Thanasis pressed a hand to the side of her head and swooped a kiss to her mouth. Green eyes glimmering, he said, 'I will be back before you have time to miss me.' And then he kissed her again, a hard, almost possessive kiss that left her seeing stars long after he'd disappeared into his room.

It was as she was swimming back to her own room that another concrete memory hit Lucie. It had to be the day she'd met Thanasis for the first time because he'd been standing with Alexis by a dark hotel bar. Other than the bartender, they'd been the only people in there. Both had been watching the door, waiting for her arrival.

She remembered the smell of the bar. Wine. A subtle but significant difference from the scent of stale beer she'd grown used to during her nights out in her six years living permanently in London.

She'd been excited to meet him. She remembered that too. Could feel the fizzing anticipation that had filled her as she'd walked through the door to him.

And she remembered how their eyes had locked together and the stunned flare of recognition on his face. The fizzing joy had almost spilled out of her to realise he too remembered that chance brief encounter from six years before. That he remembered *her*.

# CHAPTER TEN

THANASIS'S LUNGS WAITED until Sephone had disappeared on the horizon before opening fully. He was quite sure Lucie had watched the helicopter until it was nothing but a dot in the distant sky.

He put his head back and closed his eyes. He'd hated disappointing her by refusing to let her come with him, and it disturbed him just how *much* he'd hated disappointing her, but he couldn't risk having her in Athens until after the wedding. Couldn't risk her memories being triggered before he had the chance to explain everything to her.

The biggest truth though, another truth he could not share with her, was that he needed space away from her because he didn't know how much longer he could do this.

He wanted her with a desperation he'd never known it was possible to feel. He wanted all of her. Forget any future wife. No one could make him feel a fraction of what Lucie made him feel. That truth had hit him first in the chapel when he'd tried to picture the ideal wife of his future and then tried to picture marrying her in that same chapel. He'd failed to conjure any face but Lucie's. It was a truth that had solidified watching the sunset with her. Lucie was the only woman he wanted. The only wife he wanted.

Somehow he had to make it through to the wedding and pray that her dream about Athena wasn't the start of her memories returning. If that dream expanded into a full-blown memory before he had the chance to explain everything to her...

The confession he'd known he must make since he'd agreed to this charade had changed since he'd first envisaged making it. Initially, he'd imagined himself laying all the facts on the table and, while not exactly relishing the shock that was bound to follow, being unmoved by any histrionics. It had been Lucie's own fault, after all, that the need to lie to her had been deemed necessary by any of them.

To envisage his confession now, to imagine her shock, to imagine her *hurt*...

It was enough to fill his guts with an acidic dread that spread into every inch of him.

Lucie sat on the soft sandy beach of the cove nearest the villa late that afternoon, binoculars she'd managed to pilfer from a member of Thanasis's staff glued to her face. She was watching the little white dot on the horizon grow bigger. It was a yacht, a very large yacht, and it was clearly headed towards Sephone.

Who could it be? she wondered. Thanasis had mentioned there would be around fifty yachts moored around the island for the wedding, but she'd assumed they'd all be arriving either Friday—tomorrow—or on the wedding day itself.

The yacht was coming closer. Could it be one of the singers who'd be performing for them? It looked like the kind of vessel a particular world-famous diva was often photographed sunning herself on surrounded by all her sycophants. Or maybe it was one of the tech billionaires named on the guest list she'd pored over earlier? Or any of the billionaires listed, she supposed. Owning a floating palace was pretty much part of the billionaire job description, and she was very grateful for it, having spent many wonderful months of her childhood partying and having fun on Georgios's. Mostly fun, in any case. If Athena was in an accepting mood then everything would be great. If she was in one of her bitchy moods then Lucie had known it was safer to stay in her cabin. The Tsaliki males, including her brother Loukas, had all been good company but without Athena by her side she'd never been able to properly relax, had always felt she had to try too hard to be a good sport about all the boyish pranks and japes.

A sudden thought struck her and made her stomach plummet. What if it was Athena with her current beau— Athena *always* had a current beau—on that yacht?

Something unpleasant had happened between her and Athena since Lucie's engagement to Thanasis. She was certain of it. Certain too, having thought about it incessantly since he'd flown off to Athens, that Thanasis knew it too and was trying to protect her from it.

The call of her name shook her out of her thoughts, and she turned her head to find the butler heading to her with a message from Thanasis. Friends of his were arriving early and had invited them to dine on their yacht that evening, and could she please be ready to leave at eight p.m.

Well, that explained the yacht, she thought, cheering right up, and with the same fizz in her veins that had filled her all those months ago when she'd walked through the door to meet her fiancé for the first time, Lucie danced back to the villa and up to her bedroom and through to her dressing room to find something to wear for their first real date since all her memories had been wiped.

Thanasis splashed off the foam from his neck and face and patted himself dry.

Towel hung loose around his waist, he strolled into his dressing room and soon he was dressed in smart dark chinos and a black shirt he left unbuttoned at the throat.

He could have kissed Leander for arriving early and for his invitation to join them that evening. It meant he got the pleasure of Lucie's company without the torture of being alone with her. He might even allow himself a drink, something he hadn't dared since her first night here when the wine had lowered his defences and set this whole damn ball of the Lucie rollercoaster rolling.

If he was being truthful, that ball had been rolling since she'd screeched away from him in his Porsche. Maybe even since she'd bounced into that hotel bar.

The coldness he'd experienced when told she'd been in an accident should have been the warning shot he'd needed that his feelings for her ran much deeper than basic lust.

Too late now, he thought grimly, and then shook the grimness off. His attitude had ruined too many evenings for Lucie before, even if she didn't remember them. This one he would make special for her. After all, come the morning, the wedding madness would start in earnest. Lucie's bridesmaids would arrive, as would Thanasis's groomsmen, and, as a sop to the old English tradition, he and Lucie would go their separate ways and avoid each other until the wedding itself, one of the many details planned to fool the world into believing that this marriage was real.

He would not allow himself to think tonight of how much he now wanted it to be real too. He didn't dare, not when the confession he must make hung like a dark cloud over him.

A little wax in his hair and a dab of his cologne and he was good to go.

He knocked on her door.

Within moments his senses were engulfed with the scent that most drove him wild…and then he saw her standing there.

A whistle he had no control of escaped through his teeth.

Her teeth grazed her bottom lip and she gave the shy smile he hadn't seen since her first night on his island. 'Well? Will I do?'

*Do?*

All the good his day away from her had done him had evaporated. All the fortifications he'd built in his mind to get through the next few days…vanquished.

Her usual black attire was gone. In its place, a sheer jade wrap dress with spaghetti straps that plunged between her breasts and tied at the waist, heavy jade embroidery threading in a leafy pattern from the breasts and down to the loose hemline below her knees. It was sexy and tantalising without being revealing, and had the touch of bohemian to it that only Lucie could pull off. Only Lucie could pull off the curly black pineapple on her head too, but even thinking of it as that was to do it an injustice when the soft curls framed her face and enhanced her beauty and the beauty of the deep red pear drop earrings in a way that was, to his eyes, a work of art. A tendril had come loose by her left ear, a long ringlet that brushed against her shoulder and filled him with envy that it wasn't his mouth brushing against that silken skin.

He fought the groan drawing up his throat and clenched his fists to stop them cupping those beautiful cheeks and pulling that beautiful face to him.

Thrumming in him was the deep certainty that should he kiss the delectable mouth painted a tantalising deep dusky colour that was neither pink nor red but, like everything else with this incredible woman, uniquely Lucie, he would never come up for air again.

'Well?' There was a touch of anxiety in her stare.

He blew out a long breath. 'You look beautiful. You *are* beautiful.'

Her smile would have blown out any air he had left in him.

Only when she stepped closer did he realise she was wearing red heels that lifted her height enough that she didn't have to crane her neck all the way back to look in his eyes.

The hand that touched his cheeks contained a tremor in it. 'You've shaved.'

He caught the hand and, fool that he was, pressed it tighter to his skin. 'Do you approve?'

Another smile. 'You always look gorgeous.'

Incapable of releasing her hand, he lowered it and threaded his fingers through hers, then brought it to his mouth to kiss the delicate tips. 'Truly, *matia mou*. You are ravishing.' He laughed to release the tension tight in his chest. 'I'd assumed you only owned black clothes.'

'I've not worn this for you before?'

'No.' He'd never seen her wear anything like it. For their public dates together she'd always looked beautiful—hell, she always looked beautiful, whatever the time of day and whatever she was wearing—but this was the first time he'd ever felt that she'd dressed with him in mind.

'Good. Obviously I don't remember, but I didn't think I could have. I've no memory of buying it.'

When he thought of all the big memories her amnesia had taken from her, there was no reason why her failure to remember buying one dress should make him feel so wretched.

He gently fingered the loose ringlet and inhaled through his nose, filling his senses with the scent that was a manifestation of his addiction to her. 'Once the wedding is done with, I will do everything in my power to help your memories come back to you. I swear.'

The Aphrodite smile shone up at him.

Even with the sun having set, it was still hot outside, the breeze created in the buggy welcome as his driver zipped them to the harbour where a tender was waiting to sail them to Leander and Kate's yacht. Sephone had limited spots for large vessels and with Thanasis determined to leave as much of the island and its coastline untouched as he could, his refusal to dredge and create more space meant most sea-faring guests would be anchoring at sea.

He'd let go of Lucie's hand. To keep holding it was to torture himself.

From the way Lucie had pressed herself away from him, it was a suffering she shared. The airy way she was asking her questions—they were playing yet an-other round of Getting to Know You—betrayed it too. Her voice was too airy, like she was trying too hard to be carefree.

'Which of your family is the most likely to accept me?' she asked for her third question, the first two of which had been light and innocuous, and his heart sank to guess this was the question she had most wanted to ask and to know it must be playing on her mind. Wor-rying her.

'My sister.'

'How come?'

'My mother's loyalty is with my father. She will follow his lead. He's a good man—a great man—but he can be stubborn. Lydia is more open-minded, and, like a certain someone else I know, does not like being told how or what to think.' He thought of how subdued Lydia had been when the negative press had imploded their lives. He'd thought the news of the wedding and its real potential to save them all would bring some of her spark back but she'd only become more withdrawn, and he kicked himself for not having checked in on her since Lucie's accident. The truth was, his mind and his time had been entirely focused on Lucie.

*Theos*, give him the strength to make it through to the wedding.

'They will all accept you,' he vowed. 'Once they get to know you, they will learn to love you.' He would make damn sure of it.

They'd arrived at the harbour.

To Lucie's relief, Leander and Kate were two of the nicest and most welcoming people in the world. Unlike most of the uber-rich, they didn't start off their acquaintance by insisting on a tour of their yacht, something Lucie had found incredibly irksome as an adolescent whenever she'd joined the rest of the Tsaliki clan on one of Georgios's friends' vessels. Those tours were always, always designed to impress on guests just how much money and fabulous taste the host had. It would've been quicker for them to hand over their bank account statements and a listing of all expenses.

Mercifully, there was none of that with their hosts that evening. They greeted them with smiles and kisses and a bottle of champagne, and took them straight up to the sundeck without finding the need to wax lyrical about either the exact number of crystals in the chandeliers or the thread count of the thick carpet in the saloon.

The table had been set with high-class dining perfection but there was none of the formality Lucie had expected, the staff unobtrusive and polite without being fawning, Leander taking it on himself to be in charge of the drinks—Lucie quickly discovered he made a mean cocktail—and Kate, who was nearly as short as Lucie, taking it on herself to be chief taster of them.

With a variety of meze dishes to feast on and loud music playing and the stars above them twinkling, Lucie found herself relaxing in a way she hadn't expected, relaxing and laughing and generally having an excellent time.

'I hear you're an interior designer,' Kate said to Lucie after Leander had presented them each with a fresh cocktail.

Slightly embarrassed at what must seem a frivolous occupation considering Kate was a vet who'd studied for years to pursue her passion of working with orphaned orangutangs, she nodded and took a sip of her Espresso Martini.

But she really had loved her job. Loved how each job was different but how the end result always gave the same sense of satisfaction, whether it was a subtle room design or the full-blown transformation of an entire house or apartment. Loved feeling she was contributing to Kelly Holden Design steadily taking more and more lucrative business from the bigger boys.

'Which university did you study it at?'

'I didn't.'

To her surprise, Kate grinned. 'Good for you. I swear I nearly gave myself an ulcer from the stress I put myself under at university. How did you manage to get your foot in the door?'

'I took a punt… Have you heard of Kelly Holden?'

Kate shook her head. 'Should I have?'

Lucie laughed. 'Of course not. She's a goddess to me though. I always knew I wanted to do something creative, but it wasn't until I read an interview with her after her firm won this really prestigious industry award no one thought she had a chance of winning as her firm was so small and new, that I thought, yep, I want to do that and I want to work for her.'

'Just like that?'

'Just like that.'

'That's amazing—it's really similar to why I decided I had to work with orangutangs, except mine was a TV documentary. So what came next—how did you get her to take you on? Was there a lot of competition for the job?'

'I collected my final exam results from school and went straight to her offices and parked myself in the reception room for three hours until she appeared, and then

I ambushed her. God knows how I did it but I managed to convince her that what she really wanted to do was take on a green eighteen-year-old with zero experience and one A level in art as her apprentice.'

Leander lifted his glass. 'To always following your dreams.' His gaze darted to his wife, one of many secret, unspoken messages Lucie had noticed pass between them.

Theirs was the kind of relationship she longed for with Thanasis, a future she could feel them inching towards...

'Are you still working for her?' Kate asked, pulling Lucie back to the present.

'No, I had to resign... Not that I remember resigning,' she joked, even as her heart panged again at having had to walk away from the job she'd loved so much. Of all the expected guests at their wedding, Kelly was the one she was most looking forward to seeing. 'But Kelly's in London and I'm in Greece. It's just not feasible for me to stay, and interior design is not a job that lends itself to home working.' She glanced at Thanasis and, remembering his comment about no business talk at the wedding, gave a mischievous wink and said, 'I might just ask Kelly at the wedding if she'll consider expanding into Greece.'

He grinned, that gorgeous, gorgeous grin, and idly traced a finger around the rim of his glass. 'You don't need Kelly. You can set up on your own.'

'With what? I've got no money.' At the three identically shocked expressions, she laughed. 'I've supported myself since I was eighteen. I earned decent money but living in London is hugely expensive. I think I've managed to save about two hundred quid in the last six years.'

'I'll be your backer.'

She blinked, completely taken aback. It would never have occurred to her to ask Thanasis, just as she would never have thought of asking either of her parents or any of her ultra-wealthy stepfamily. 'I couldn't ask that of you, but thank you.'

'You're not asking, I'm offering.'

'And it's a lovely offer but I've always had an aversion to being in debt—I borrowed a hundred euros off Athena once and she harangued me until every last cent had been repaid, and then wouldn't let me forget how kind and generous she'd been to me.' Those one hundred euros had been to cover Lucie's share of the bill on a night out for her own birthday at an expensive club where Athena had insisted on taking her to celebrate it.

His smile and accompanying laughter didn't quite meet the serious hue in his eyes. 'We can discuss it after the wedding, but what I will point out now is that once we're married, everything I have is yours, so you can never be indebted to me.'

'No more boring work talk or I will get the baby photos out,' Leander interrupted with a grin. 'Now, who wants to try a Coquito?'

Was she drunk? Lucie wondered as she embraced Kate and Leander and thanked them again for a wonderful evening. She felt drunk, but not *drunk* drunk. Not like she had that night with Athena when she'd been fifteen.

This was a different kind of drunkenness, one oiled a little by cocktails but fuelled by the joy of being alive.

In less than two days she would be married to this gorgeous man holding her with such secure rigidity to him as their tender sped them back to the harbour. He would be her husband and she would be his wife and the whole future would be theirs for the taking.

# CHAPTER ELEVEN

THANASIS'S CHEST HAD never felt so tight.

Far from their evening with Leander and Kate giving him space to breathe whilst enjoying Lucie's company, all it had done was bind him closer to her. Bind him closer to the truth of her, which was that Lucie was the fiercest, funniest, most unique person in the entire world.

It was a truth that had been peeling away in slow increments since Lucie had screeched away from his house in utter distress, but he'd been too blind to see her anger for what it had really been. He'd seen what he'd wanted to see. Seen what he'd needed to see.

Too blind to accept the truth.

He'd been in love with her from the start.

He suspected she'd been in love with him from the start too.

They rode in silence back to the villa he already knew he could not imagine living in without her.

He needed to think and work out what the hell he was going to do. God damn it, they were marrying in two days.

Inside, she reached for his hand.

'Thanasis...'

The emotions spilled over. Clasping her cheeks, he kissed her deeply, pouring into it all his passion and desire for her and selfishly helping himself to a taste of her passion and desire for him.

He broke away and gazed intently into the stunned black eyes. 'I love you, Lucie. Now get some sleep and we will talk in the morning.'

He took the stairs two at a time, her dazed stare following his every step.


Lucie pressed her back to the nearest wall and her hand to her heart.

Her legs felt like soggy noodles.

The butler appeared. Offered her a drink.

'Your smoothest Scotch,' she whispered. 'No ice.'

She swallowed it in one and then looked up the winding staircase.

The liquid medicine wound its way into her chest and with it came the clarity she'd been searching for.

All her life Lucie had known that to get what she wanted, she had to work at it and take it for herself because no one else was going to help her. She'd never *wanted* anyone's help. Everything she'd achieved in her life had come off her own hard work, so why was she still letting Thanasis dictate all the terms when she'd resisted being dictated to since hitting double digits?

Because deep down had been the fear that he was right and none of her feelings were real.

But they *were* real. As real as the air she was breathing and as real as the cool tiles beneath her feet.

He wanted her. She wanted him. He loved her...

She laughed.

He'd never said those words before. Not to post-amnesia Lucie.

Kicking her shoes off, she ran up the stairs.

Thanasis stripped off his shirt in front of the mirror. He swore he could see the thrashing of his heart against his chest.

He unzipped his chinos and let them fall to the floor.

He felt sick. Sick with himself. Sick with what he had to do and what the ramifications could be.

He needed to press the nuclear button.

He couldn't marry her. Not like this. Lucie deserved to know the truth before they made their vows.

But not now. In the morning. First thing in the morning. Let her have peace for one more night before her peace of mind was shattered for ever. He owed her that much.

So caught up was he in his despairing thoughts that the first tap on his door didn't penetrate.

It was the hairs rising on the back of his neck that told him.

On legs that didn't feel like they belonged to him, he crossed the room.

He could smell her perfume before his hand touched the door.

Swallowing hard, he opened it, and then sucked in a breath.

It was the last breath he was capable of making for a long, long time.

Lucie was naked.

Heaven help him, she was fully, proudly naked and far more beautiful than his wildest imaginings, her chin lifted, her hair loose and as wild as the expression in her eyes.

She took a step towards him.

Oh, God help him.

'Lucie…' He lifted a hand to ward her off and tried to speak through his clenched teeth. *'Please.'*

She took the hand gently with both of hers and placed it flat on her left breast. Held it there.

His fingers reflexively tightened around it even as he fought harder than ever to hold on. *Theos*, he could feel the heavy thrum of her heart. Feel the jut of her nipple against his palm, not a whisper of barrier between them.

He closed his eyes and groaned. Blood was pounding in his head.

God help him, please.

Lucie drank Thanasis in with a greed she'd never known was possible. To see the rise and fall of his chest and the expression in the green eyes before he'd closed them to her…

She rose onto her toes and palmed his cheek.

His nostrils flared.

'Lucie…' His voice was ragged. Tortured. 'Please. Go back to your room. We *can't.*'

Thick stubble had sprung out on skin that only hours ago had been baby smooth from his shave, and the pads of her fingers tingled madly in reaction to the sharpness. Her longing for him intensified.

Slowly sliding her fingers across his jaw and down the strong throat, touching him as she'd done so many times in her fantasies, she whispered, 'I might not have past memories to pin my feelings on, but I do have my heart and my gut, and both have been telling me since I woke in that hospital bed that you mean something to me. Those feelings have only grown stronger.' She trailed her trembling fingers over his chest and tipped her nose into the base of his neck to breathe in the musky scent of his skin.

Other than the flexing of his fingers over her breast, he'd barely moved a muscle, but she could feel the internal battle he was waging against himself and it filled her thrashing heart with fresh tenderness for him.

Excitement building, she skimmed her fingers over the plane of his hard abdomen and thrilled over his latent power.

It felt like she'd been waiting her whole life for this moment.

His throat moved. She pressed a kiss to it before tilting her head back and cupping his cheeks, willing him to look at her.

Tremulously, she said, 'I saw you across that room all those years ago and something moved in me, and I have carried it in me all this time. I don't want to wait any more. I want *you*, Thanasis, the man I've got to know here, exactly as you are here with me right now.'

Thanasis's groan escaped his mouth before he could stop it and, before he could stop himself, his hand fell away from Lucie's breast to slide behind her back and his hungry lips fused hard against hers.

The relief at finally letting himself go was dizzying, and he held her even tighter to him and kissed her even harder, groaning as her breasts pressed against him and her arms slid around his neck, the passion in her response scorching him with a heat that melted the last of the mental shackles binding him and unleashed all his hunger in one long surge of passion.

He couldn't fight something this strong and this essential. God help him, he needed her, needed Lucie with a hunger he'd never believed existed.

Let her feel it all, all his passion and love for her. Let her feel everything she was and everything she meant to him.

Lucie sank into the ravenous kiss with a sob of pleasure, her lips parting as her senses overloaded with the dark, addictively intoxicating taste and scent of Thanasis. Flames erupted inside her, licking her into a furnace and liquefying her, and it was all she could do to bite her fingers into his neck to hold herself upright and sink even deeper into the possessive demands of his mouth.

Without a single word being uttered, he swept her into his arms and carried her to the bed. There, he laid her down and then, his hooded eyes fixed on her, removed his underwear…heavens, he was *huge*…and climbed on top of her.

For the longest time he just stared at her, breathing heavily, drinking her in as if she were the goddess of his dreams.

The swell of muscles in his shoulders bunching as he supported his weight to lower himself onto her gave another hint of his innate masculine power, and the most feminine part of her revelled to see it and thrilled to see the wonder in his stare. If there had been so much as a fleck of doubt that she was doing the right thing, it had vanished. This was exactly where she was supposed to be. In Thanasis's arms and in his bed.

And then their mouths fused back together, hot and greedy, a primitive hunger that burned through sense and logic and burned through the last of her thoughts.

Wrapping her arms around his neck, Lucie scratched her nails into the soft bristles at the nape, closing her eyes and her mind to everything but the sensory pleasure of Thanasis, keeping them closed when his mouth moved from hers and razed its way down her neck, would have cried her disappointment when he left her neck if he hadn't cupped her breast and sent a gasp flying from her lips, a gasp that turned into a sob when his mouth closed over the tip.

She was on fire, writhing with him and against him, her body gripped with such intense excitement it was impossible to still herself until he clasped hold of her wrists. Flames were licking her skin, heat bubbling deep within her, no longer some distant squirmy feeling between her legs but a pulse beating hard, and when his tongue licked and then suckled, rousing her nipples into hard peaks that had her whispering incoherently, the pulse tightened and she instinctively arched into his mouth.

The grip on her wrists didn't lessen as he snaked his way lower, and she spread her thighs for him without a moment of hesitation, surrendering herself to him in her entirety, desperate for the ache between her thighs to be relieved, and when his tongue found her swollen arousal, any sense she had left in her was lost in the thrills of what Thanasis was doing to her.

The flames were suffusing her, throbbing and pulsing, building into something entirely and solely within his control, and she cried out to him, pleading and begging until she spiralled over the edge and spasms of unrelenting pleasure flooded her with a force that sent white light flickering behind her eyes.

By the time the earth reclaimed her and she blinked her eyes open, there was no time to recover before Thanasis crawled up her body to kiss her, and suddenly her mouth was filled with an exotic taste…her taste.

Fresh hunger filled her and suddenly she was consumed with the need to worship him with the same heady attention he'd just gifted her, and she pushed at his chest to roll him onto his back.

With the taste of Lucie's climax still on his tongue, Thanasis submitted to an assault of his senses that would have lost him his mind if it wasn't already gone. Every touch and mark of her mouth and tongue scorched him. Never had he been on the receiving end of such pleasure, but it was much more than that, more than a bodily experience, this transcended everything…

He groaned and had to grit his teeth when she took hold of his erection, then gritted them even harder when she took him in her mouth.

He lifted his head to look at her at the same moment her gaze lifted to his.

His heart punched through him to see the desire-laden wonder in her stare.

Closing his eyes, he gathered her hair lightly and let her take the lead, throwing his head back on the pillow as her movements, tentative at first, became emboldened. The fist she'd made around the base tightened and she took him deeper into her mouth, moaning her own pleasure at the pleasure she was giving him.

If heaven existed he'd just found it. This was like nothing…nothing…

The telltale tug of his orgasm began to pull at him, and with an exhale of air, he flipped her back round, pulling her up the bed to pin her back beneath him.

Throat too constricted to speak, he kissed her deeply, the tip of his erection jutting and straining against her slick heat.

Lucie felt possessed, that there was every chance she would go insane if Thanasis didn't take possession of her. She had never wanted anything as badly as she wanted this. Every inch of her body was alight with the flames he'd ignited, her senses consumed with him. His beautiful face was all she could see, his ragged breaths all she could hear, his musky skin all she could smell and all she could taste, the smoothness of his skin all she could feel.

Shivering with longing, she rocked her hips, encouraging his possession, her breathing rapid as he stilled himself to drive into her, and with a long, drawn-out groan he was deeply and fully inside her and it was the most incredible sensation she could have dreamed of.

Limbs and tongues entwined, he drove in and out of her, the burn in her core reigniting and deepening and then uncoiling like tendrils through her very being until she was nothing but a mass of nerve endings, and the burning pressure deep inside of her exploded.

With a long cry, she buried her mouth into his neck and held tight as rolling waves of bliss flooded her. Somewhere in the recesses of her mind, she heard Thanasis shout out, and then there was one last furious thrust that locked their groins together for one final time.

Buried as deep inside Lucie as he'd ever dreamed it was possible to be, Thanasis felt his climax roar through him. And still he tried to bury deeper, still she tried to pull him deeper, both of them desperately drawing out the pleasure for as long as they could until there was nothing left but stunned silence.

Thanasis, eyes closed, stroked the smooth back of the woman cuddled so tightly into him. Their legs were entwined, her soft curls tickling his throat and chin.

If not for the weight in his heart, this would be the deepest contentment he'd ever known.

He'd never experienced anything like that before. Nothing close. That had transcended *everything*.

He pressed a kiss into her hair and breathed her in, wishing they could just stay like this.

A little longer. Let them have this moment. Let all the feelings seep through them and work their magic long enough that when he made the confession that he must, Lucie would understand their lovemaking had been separate from everything else.

God, please make her understand.

She sighed and then lifted her head to rest her chin on his chest. 'I'm hungry.'

He ran a finger through a curl and smiled to watch it magically turn into three separate curls. 'You're always hungry… What did you eat while I was in Athens?'

'Not much. Elias made me a couple of flatbreads with that lovely feta and yogurt mousse.'

'Again?' They'd only had that for their lunch the day before. Each flatbread was the size of a dinner plate.

She gave him that mischievous grin but her eyes were still soft from their lovemaking. 'I asked him very nicely. Oh, and I had a bowl of pistachio ice cream too, which I think is the nicest ice cream I've ever had. I would seriously advise locking him away for the wedding or one of your guests is going to steal him.'

His throat constricted. He swallowed hard to clear it. 'I will give your advice the serious consideration it deserves.'

'Good. Because if you don't, you'll need a new wife as I'll be off tracking Elias down.'

Now his heart constricted too before expanding heavily, compressing him with its weight, a sluggish pulse beating in his head.

'Are you okay?'

Lucie's voice seemed to come from far away but her face had closed in, concerned black eyes hovering right before him.

'Earth to Thanasis.' Her concern was mirrored in her tone and it came to him with a sickening thud that he didn't deserve her concern.

Reverently tracing the line of her jaw, he gazed into the most beautiful eyes in the world and knew the moment he'd wanted to stretch for eternity was already over.

'There is something I need to tell you. Something you need to know.'

Her forehead creased.

'Lucie…' He closed his eyes briefly before fixing them back to hers. 'What I'm about to tell you… Know that I love you. Hold that thought. I love you.'

Apprehension written all over her face, she lifted herself up, hugging the sheets to her breasts. 'You're scaring me,' she whispered.

'I'm sorry.' Deep in the very pit of his being, the weight of dread was pulling at him. His next words would determine the remaining course of his life. 'I'm sorry, Lucie, but our past, what you've been told, it's all a lie. You and I were never in love.'

For the longest time she just sat there looking at him blankly. And then she seemed to shrink, the colour draining from her face, eyes dulling with comprehension.

'Forgive me,' he said quietly, knowing as he said it that he didn't deserve her forgiveness, 'but we were never lovers. We were as far from lovers as it is possible for two people to be.'

# CHAPTER TWELVE

LUCIE SAW THANASIS'S lips move but heard no sound above the roar in her head.

Time had faded away, the world spinning around her and then ebbing to a crawl, everything that had happened between them since she'd woken in her hospital bed flashing like picture stills in her vision.

Slowly, slowly, the present began to weave back into her consciousness, her eyes clearing to soak in the dark stubble on Thanasis's jawline, and the dark hairs of his chest which were so soft in stark contrast to the hardness of the muscle and bone beneath them, the nerves of her hand registering the tenderness of the giant hands holding hers… She had no recollection of him taking them or even of him sitting up to face her. She heard, too, the tenderness in his voice.

'Lucie, say something, please.'

Her head was pounding.

Slowly, she forced herself to meet his stare.

His green eyes were stark with torment.

She tugged her hands free and whispered, 'I need to use the bathroom.'

Twisting to the edge of the bed, she groped with her foot for the floor then fought to keep her legs upright as she staggered away from him, suddenly aware that she was cold. Cold and naked.

Naked from their lovemaking.

A whimper rose up her throat but she smothered it, dragging her legs to the door he'd silently indicated, suddenly desperate to cover her nakedness.

Oh, dear God help her, had it *all* been a lie?

There was a grey robe on the door but she couldn't bring herself to touch it, and she wrapped a bath towel around herself before splashing water on her clammy face.

She was shaking. Her whole body.

The memory she'd been searching for finally flashed before her. Lucie and her mother alone in her hospital room.

*'Mum, how do Thanasis and I get on? The nurse seems to think...'*

*'Seems to think what?'*

*'She thinks he's in love with me.'*

*'It has been obvious to us all that strong emotions have developed between you.'*

But her mum hadn't met Thanasis before Lucie's accident. It had been a lie. One of many, many lies.

She rammed her fist into her mouth to smother the scream fighting to break free.

Oh, God, how could she face seeing him again?

She *had* to face him. There was no other choice.

When she finally left the bathroom, he'd thrown on a

pair of shorts and was sitting at the end of the bed rubbing his head.

She sank her weak legs onto an armchair facing him and forced herself to meet his gaze. 'Was any of it true? You and me? The great unexpected romance?'

There was a bleakness in his stare. 'No. None of it was true. It was a lie we fed you to stop you leaving me again.'

She gripped hold of her knees and hung her head in an effort to fight against a world trying to spin itself off its axis around her again. 'Again?'

He gave a taut nod. 'I hated you. I made your life a misery.'

She turned her face away, his blunt admittance slicing like a knife through her heart.

The spasm of pain on Lucie's face lanced him. Drawing in a long breath, Thanasis filled himself with resolve.

She deserved the truth.

And he deserved whatever retribution came from it.

Especially now.

God forgive him.

'I hated your entire family. I agreed to the marriage because it was the only viable way of saving my business and saving my family from destitution, but I hated you before I even set eyes on you and when I did set eyes on you and realised you were the woman from the party I'd searched the streets of Athens for, I made damned sure that you hated me too.'

Her gaze turned back to him, her distressed black eyes wide.

'Oh, yes,' Thanasis said grimly. 'I was deliberate about it. I had mentally allocated two years of my life to our marriage, and then it would be dissolved and I would find myself a real wife to build my real future with. Georgios Tsaliki's stepdaughter was never going to be that woman.'

God that he could take it all back. Rewind to when he'd opened his bedroom door to find her naked and tell her the truth then, before he'd lost himself to the heat of his passion for her and shared the most incredible and fulfilling emotional and physical experience of his life with the woman whose heart had connected to his and which he now needed to break.

He could only pray that Lucie could find it in herself to forgive him. He would never forgive himself.

'In my wildest, most secret dreams, the woman I would build my future with was the tiny waif with a mass of black curly hair who'd captured a piece of my heart all those years ago...'

Her chin wobbled. She made the smallest of whimpers.

God that he could lift all her pain from her. He would not close his eyes or his ears to it.

'And then I found she was you.' His mouth twisted in self-loathing. 'I cannot tell you how much I hated you for being her, or how much I hated myself for still wanting you. I even hated you for your selflessness—you were giving up your life and independence to save the fortunes of a monster and getting nothing in return. You asked for nothing in return. Nothing.

'You and I spent two months in a war I instigated and fed. I treated you despicably and in turn you treated me with loathing and contempt, but to reiterate—it all came from me. You'd been prepared to give me a chance... I'd seen it in your eyes and I hated that about you too. This was all on me. Everything that was toxic about our relationship came from me, and I will regret my behaviour and the way I treated you for the rest of my life.'

She closed her eyes.

*Theos*, she looked so small. So lost. The towel she'd wrapped around herself was swallowing her up.

If only she would let him reach across...

Her eyes opened and clamped onto his. 'What happened at the end?'

His stomach lurched. He pulled his lips together.

'What else?' she said, her voice hardening. 'I know there's something else and I know it involves Athena.'

Of all the things he'd never wanted Lucie to relive, this had been at the top of his list.

To relive it meant she would have to relive her pain and distress.

But he couldn't hide it from her or try and sweeten it. The truth he owed her was the full truth.

If he'd been a better man, he'd have said to hell with consequences and told her the full truth a week ago.

But a week ago he hadn't known he loved her. Hadn't known Lucie's happiness and peace of mind would come to mean more to him than anything.

'Did you sleep with her?'

He didn't drop his stare. 'No, but she led you to believe that I did.'

Whatever little colour that had returned to her cheeks vanished.

'When we first discussed marriage between the two families, it was agreed, at my suggestion, that I would marry Athena—she was Georgios's only blood daughter so it made sense to me. But just as I wouldn't entertain Alexis marrying Lydia, Georgios refused to let Athena marry me. Marrying you was at his suggestion. The fact the world has always regarded you as his daughter meant our marriage would have the same effect. At some point Athena learned she'd been first choice.' Now he did close his eyes. 'She came to me.'

'Came to you?' she croaked. 'What does that mean?'

'She came to my offices.' He forced himself to look back at her. 'After everything about the marriage was agreed and you moved to Greece, you spent a lot of time with her. She knew you and I hated each other and seemed to think my suggestion of marriage to her meant that I must want her. She tried to seduce me.'

A pulse was throbbing in the base of her throat. 'Tried?'

'Yes. Tried. She kissed my neck, I pushed her away and told her to leave. She left. The first I knew that she'd gone straight to the apartment to see you was when I got home. You were waiting for me. You checked the collar of my shirt, saw the lipstick mark she'd left on it and that was it. You hit the roof. You refused to let me explain myself. You stole my car keys out of my hand and told me the wedding was off.'

'I didn't believe you?'

'You wouldn't let me speak to explain. You were in a terrible state.' He took a deep breath. 'I thought then that it was anger but it was distress. I think Athena hurt you very much. The things she said to you. She told you about Georgios insisting that you be the one to make the sacrifice of marriage for the sake of the family. Told you why.'

Her pretty eyebrows had drawn together. 'Why would Athena do that to me? Our relationship has always been fractious but I never thought she hated me.'

'She is poisonous.'

'She's been a sister to me since I was three years old.'

'Sisters because your mother stole her father from her mother.'

Her eyes squeezed shut.

'In Athena's eyes, it is the truth,' he said.

'But I was a *child*.'

'Her mother is poison. The whole Tsaliki family and anyone who marries into them is poison or becomes contaminated by it. They are all selfish and out for themselves—it is why our fathers fell out and separated the business into two. My father learned Georgios was taking bribes. Athena saw a chance to hurt you and she took it. To her, it was a bit of mindless entertainment to ease the boredom of her life. She had no care for your feelings because she is incapable of caring for anyone but herself.'

'Then you should have taken what she was offering because you have no care for my feelings either,' she whispered.

'Your feelings matter more to me than anything.'

Her gaze levelled back on him. 'Oh, I think I'm as expendable to you as I so clearly am to everyone else.'

'Don't say that.'

'Why not? We're speaking truths, aren't we? You let me believe you were holding back from me because you didn't want to take advantage of my missing memories...' Lucie closed her eyes, fighting with everything she had to hold on to her composure.

She'd instigated their lovemaking. *She* had. Not Thanasis. Right until the very end, he'd fought away from it.

Oh, God, she couldn't bear to remember how beautiful it had been. How beautiful he had made her feel. How *loved* he'd made her feel.

She'd given him everything she had to give and all along...

She'd thought she'd been taking control but she was the one who'd been controlled, right from the moment she'd woken up in that hospital bed.

She snapped her gaze back to him. 'I'm sure you can soothe your conscience by telling yourself that you *tried* to resist the chemistry between us, and, quite honestly, I can imagine living with you *was* like living in a form of war zone. I'm a prickly bear when people are mean to me—you lash out at me and if I've got nowhere to hide then I lash right back, and I know perfectly well that if you of all people had been cruel to me then my self-defence mechanism would have kicked in, and when I say you of all people I mean it's because I spent six years painting you in my head as this romantic hero, luckily not to the extent where I fancied myself in love with you or anything, but enough that it would have hurt to learn you really were the unmitigated bastard the Tsalikis always painted you as being, and I am trying so hard right now not to lash out at you and call you every vile name under the sun for what you've done to me and for all the lies you've been feeding me...'

'I've tried very hard not to tell you outright lies.'

'Oh, aren't you a regular saint?' she scorned bitterly, needing to *be* scornful, needing to keep speaking because something was swelling inside her, pushing into her chest and throat, something hot and ugly and dripping with the pain that every word uttered by Thanasis had made her bleed with.

'Everything apart from our past has been the truth, I swear.'

'Quick, polish your halo. But as I was saying, I'm trying very hard not to call you all the vile names that are lining up on my tongue, and trying even harder not to imagine breaking your nose and, and...and...' She couldn't contain the agony a second longer. Before she could stop them, tears were pouring down her face and Lucie was on her feet and charging at him, pushing as hard as she could into Thanasis's chest to send him falling back onto the mattress, climbing on top of him, straddling him as she screamed obscenities and pounded her fists at his chest.

'How could you?' she sobbed when all her obscenities had dried up but not an ounce of the agony had been purged. 'How could you, how could you, how *could* you? How could you do that to me? I did nothing to any of you except love you and you all lied, and you, you bastard, you pretended that you loved me and cared for me when all along you hated me...'

Finally, he grabbed her wrists to control her and flipped her over, pinning her down. 'No, Lucie, I have *never* hated you, never believe that. I only thought I did, and it's only now that I look back and can see it was a lie I fed myself.'

She shook her head wildly. 'Every word out of your mouth has been a lie!'

'*No.*'

'You made me fall in love with you, and all so you could save your bastard business when you didn't even need to tell me the lie!'

'I know, but once the lie had been fed I had no choice but to go along with it.'

'You're Thanasis Antoniadis,' she screamed. 'Of course you had a choice! The only person in this whole sordid affair not given a choice is me because all the choices I made were choices based on lies because I'm the expendable one, the one who never fits in anywhere so who bloody well cares about Lucie?'

'I care, more than anything.'

'Well, I don't. I don't care about you and I don't care about the Tsalikis. You can all rot in hell together—you deserve each other, now get off me, get off me, get *off* me!'

Breathing heavily, he let go of her wrists and moved off her.

In a flash, she'd scrambled off the bed and was out of the door before Thanasis had managed to haul himself off the mattress to chase after her.

He slammed her bedroom door open. The room was empty but he could hear her throwing things around in her dressing room and snatched a tiny breath of relief that she hadn't run off naked into the night.

He stood by the door. 'Lucie, please, I know you're hurting, but please don't do anything rash. Hate me, hit me, punch me, do all the things you want, just don't go. Not like this. Stay with me. Please. Just give me a chance to put things right.'

She appeared in front of him hugging her overnight case to her chest, a broken Aphrodite with bloodshot eyes and hair like a nest and a thin black dress she'd put on back to front. 'Put things right so I'll marry you and keep the public lie going?'

'I don't care about the wedding,' he roared. 'All I care about is you, and right now I'm terrified you're going to go off and do something stupid like you did the last time.'

There was a moment of complete stillness before Lucie slowly straightened, seeming to grow and magnify before his eyes, as proud and as powerful as Hera herself.

'The only stupid thing I've done other than believe your lies is fall in love with you,' she said with deadly, ice-cold precision. 'But, believe me, I'm over that now, and if you think I'm going to do something rash that puts me in danger then you're the stupid one because you're the last person in the world I'd hurt myself over. Do not follow me, do not ever make contact with me again. I have nothing left to say to you.'

This time, Thanasis let her go.

Lucie sat on a rock by the harbour watching the sun rise. She would never now have the chance to watch it rise on the mountain's summit. Never mind. There were lots of things in life she would never get her chance at. Getting married was but one of them, and it was with that philosophical thought in mind that she got to her feet at the sight of the boat approaching the harbour with supplies for the wedding that would never take place.

An hour later she was sailing away from Sephone.

She didn't look back.

Thanasis watched the boat containing the woman he loved disappear on the horizon.

The world swayed beneath his feet and he had to squeeze his eyes shut to ground himself.

Heading in the other direction, sailing towards him, the first of the many yachts sailing to Sephone for the wedding of the century.

He rubbed at his raw, gritty eyes.

So much to do. A wedding to cancel. All the people who needed to be notified. The press, who needed to be managed.

He didn't have the heart or energy to do any of it.

It no longer mattered what he lost. He'd already lost the only thing that mattered.

This time, there would be no reprieve. No third chance. Lucie was gone for ever.

# CHAPTER THIRTEEN

THE KINDNESS OF strangers was something Lucie would never take for granted again. After docking in Kos, the captain of the supply boat, who must have thought she was some kind of castaway who'd ended up on Sephone by accident, had given her his phone and been happy for her to search the business number for Kelly Holden Design and then make a call to England. Four hours later, she had the last available ticket for a flight to London.

Her father, stepmother and half-sisters, all laden with luggage, all failed to spot her when she passed them outside the airport.

The package that had been couriered was nondescript. Just the ordinary white plastic packaging of a particular courier service. The only thing out of the ordinary was that the sender had known to send it to Kelly's house. No one other than Kelly and her husband knew Lucie had taken refuge with them. If the press found out, they would descend on the Holden home like bees around a honeypot but with a much nastier sting.

They'd been stalking Thanasis for five days. She

wished she didn't know this but Kelly had loaned her a spare laptop and, like the masochist she was, Lucie couldn't stop herself stalking his name.

He deserved everything he had coming to him, she told herself with regularly needed fortitude as she read article after article detailing the mysterious circumstances of the bride's disappearance from Sephone, and article after article about the future of Antoniadis Shipping and the severe peril it had been plunged into.

Thanasis's refusal to discuss the cancelled wedding only added fuel to a fire keeping the Internet alive with gossip and rumour. The few paparazzi shots of him showed a dishevelled man who'd stopped sleeping. Well, he wasn't going to get any sympathy from her, not when she held him responsible for the purple hollows that had appeared beneath her own eyes.

Tsaliki Shipping wasn't faring much better in the publicity stakes, and now there were rumours circulating that the missing bride had been forced by her evil stepfamily into marrying their enemy, and that she'd run away to escape her fate and was refusing to return to the Tsaliki family bosom. Her mum, Lucie thought, played the part of distressed mother quite well but she really needed to get some stronger onions to provoke better tears. As for Athena…

Athena's actions had broken her heart, more so even than her mother's had. Her mother had always been selfish and single-minded, but Athena's cruelty cut deep.

Had she always resented her? Had her sporadic mood

swings and bitchiness been symptoms of something that ran deeper than Lucie had known?

It was unlikely she'd ever know. She never wanted to see any of the Tsalikis again. None of them loved her. That was the truth. You didn't treat someone the way they'd collectively conspired to treat her if you loved them. Lucie was expendable to them. She was expendable to everyone.

The package was still in her hands.

Some kind of sixth sense told Lucie what it contained and who'd sent it: the person whose very name it destroyed her to think of. And it was because of this sixth sense that she held off opening it until night fell and she was alone in the guest room with her ninth cup of tea of the day. It was the only form of sustenance her belly could cope with. Coffee turned her stomach. All foods tightened it into a ball.

At least she wasn't pregnant. She supposed that should be considered a mercy. Certainly not something to feel wretched about. Hadn't even been something she'd given two thoughts about until her period had started that morning.

Why hadn't Thanasis used protection? It was the first time she'd dared ask herself that question. She knew why she hadn't—because she'd believed herself in love with him. Love, marriage and babies.

None of these were things she would ever have now. To love, you had to trust and she would never trust again. When she was back on her feet—Kelly had given Lucie her old job back without having to be ambushed into it—

she would rent herself a small place and get herself a cat. At least cats never pretended to be anything other than what they were. Yes. A cat. Maybe a new cat each year, create a collection of them, and then when she was an old lady and her hair all wild and grey, she would morph into the local cat lady and let that be her legacy.

She couldn't put it off any longer. Lucie ripped into the packaging. Inside was a box as nondescript as the packaging. Wrapped around the box was an envelope with her name on it written in a penmanship she didn't recognise but which still made her tremble.

She closed her eyes.

Box or envelope first?

Box.

And there it was. Her phone.

She turned it on and waited for it to power up.

Moments later and it was beeping and chirping like an aviary at feeding time.

Ninety-seven missed calls. Two hundred and nineteen text messages…

She turned it upside down so she didn't have to see them and could ignore a little longer her friends' entreaties for her to get in touch.

She would ignore any entreaties from her family for ever. Except for her dad. None of this was his fault. His only crime was to like order more than he liked his daughter, and she didn't even think it was that he didn't like her, it was more that he didn't understand her. In his own way, he did love her, and she should message and let him know she was safe.

Duty to her father done, she held the envelope in her hand.

Now she really was shaking. The palms of her hands had gone clammy.

She ripped it open and pulled out the letter contained in it.

*Dear Lucie,*

*Forgive me for going against your wishes in communicating with you, but this was recently found in my apartment's car park. I admit, returning it to you is the excuse I have been seeking to reach out to you.*

*I know that much of what I'm going to write now is not what you want to hear so I can only hope you can bring yourself to read it, but will understand if it is too much for you.*

*I have been thinking a lot about our time together on Sephone, and, Lucie, they were the best days of my life. There is something inherently joyful in your nature that sings to something in me that is usually so serious, and I pray my actions haven't destroyed this essential part of you.*

*You were right in saying I had a choice over whether to lie to you. I did have a choice and I made the wrong one. It is a choice I will regret until my dying day, and I will regret it not for what it's done to me but for what it's done to you. You didn't deserve any of this.*

*I don't know if you realised it when we were*

*dining with them, but Leander was the host of the party I first saw you at all those years ago. Seeing you at that party changed something in me. I don't believe there is such a thing as love at first sight but I have carried your image with me ever since, and now I carry you fully in my heart. You are beautiful, Lucie, inside and out, and you deserve the world. I just wish I could be the one to give it to you.*

*I'm sorry for the pain I caused you. I hope one day you find the courage to love again and I hope the man you find that courage with treats you with the respect and devotion you deserve.*

*I meant every word I said to you on the mountain.*

*I will love you for ever,*
*Thanasis*

By the time Lucie had read the letter a fifth time, the paper was soaked with her tears, her face burrowed in a pillow as all the pain and anguish she'd tried so hard to contain purged from her.

Lucie lay like a starfish, unseeing wet eyes fixed on the ceiling, the ruined letter still clutched in her hand. All those precious words dissolved. All his precious words. All dissolved as if they'd never existed...

No, that couldn't be true because they'd etched into her heart, just as the man who'd written them had, and the world turned itself back to the moment she'd first opened her eyes to find him there, and then it speeded up, reeling her through their time together until that final beautiful night, before he'd confessed the truth...

But what was the truth? That she should listen to her head and forget him? Or that she should listen to her heart, which knew she could live a thousand years and would still carry him inside its broken walls?

The only truth she knew for certain was the truth about how Thanasis made her feel, and the pain of his absence hurt a thousand times more than the pain of the loss of her mother and the entirety of her stepfamily combined.

As memories of their lovemaking danced through her mind Lucie lifted herself off the bed and opened the guest room curtains. The sun would soon be rising in Greece. Thanasis would watch it rise under a different sky from hers. And he would watch it, she knew it. He'd watch the sun rise and he would think of her. Every sunrise and sunset he saw for the rest of his life would come with memories of her because he loved her. That was another truth.

And there was one more truth. Unless she could bring herself to forgive him, she would have to endure a lifetime of sunrises and sunsets without him. She would be destined to live in perpetual winter like Demeter without Persephone, desolate and barren of heart and soul.

Thanasis showered, shaved, brushed his teeth, dressed, and styled his hair without any recollection of doing any of it. He fed muesli into his mouth. There was no point eating anything worth tasting. He couldn't taste anything. Food had become fuel, nothing more. Most aromas turned his stomach.

In the back of his car, he stretched out his legs and flicked through his notes. He'd been up until the early hours preparing. Antoniadis Shipping's major investors had demanded a meeting. In just two days, the fleet of ships would be delivered and the four billion would have to be paid. There was no guarantee that money would be available, not when the major investors were talking behind backs and working to their own agendas. He had a feeling today's meeting was nothing but a courtesy. He'd warned his parents to start looking for a smaller home. A much smaller home. His sister was refusing to take his calls. One more headache he didn't need.

The car pulled up outside his headquarters.

He rolled his neck.

Flanked by his lawyer and PA, Thanasis swept through the door and took the elevator to the top floor. Every employee he came across he greeted with his usual courtesy. He would not have anyone think he was concerned his world was about to be destroyed.

Besides, you couldn't destroy something that was already wrecked, and Thanasis's life was as wrecked as wrecked could be. If not for his family and thousands of employees, he would tell the investors to do whatever the hell they wanted to his business and then walk away from it all. There was nothing left for him. There was no life for him without Lucie. Only existence. All a man needed to exist were a roof over his head and three square meals a day.

But he would play the game one last time for his family and employees' sakes.

The walls of the boardroom were glass and he could see them already in there, plotting over good coffee and fresh pastries *he'd* provided.

He shook their hands and took his seat.

The moment Craig opened his mouth, Thanasis knew it was game over.

Words were bandied around. English word salads. Corporate jargon to justify the cowardice. He tuned most of the words out, only the odd ones floating into his consciousness. Reputational Management were his favourites. Especially coming from a man Thanasis knew for a fact was cheating on his wife with their children's nanny.

He made a half-hearted attempt to fight his corner but it was like a boxer already down on points in the final round with his opponent still fresh and bouncing in the ring.

He wondered if Lucie had found her bounce again yet. He hoped so. He prayed for her to have found her bounce again. The Lucie bounce...

The investors had stopped talking, their necks craned to a commotion occurring outside the boardroom.

Thanasis might be dead inside but he could still manage to raise one eyebrow as a sop to curiosity.

He started. Sat up straighter.

He could have sworn he'd just seen a curly black pineapple...

Just as he was blinking to clear his eyes, a tiny waif

in a long flowing black dress, black jacket with crystals studded into it and chunky black boots ducked out from the crowd and, before anyone could stop her, flung the boardroom door wide open.

'Apologies, gentlemen...lady.' She smiled widely around the room. 'I just need a quick word with my fiancé.' Then, to Thanasis, she said, 'Can you believe I forgot my security pass again? I'm so sorry. Honestly, I swear I'd forget my head if it wasn't screwed on.' Attention back on the investors, she tapped the side of her head. 'Brain injury. I do *not* recommend. But on the mend now, so all good.'

Everyone's mouth had fallen open, none wider than Thanasis's. He'd lost control of his body. He couldn't even raise his hands to rub his eyes.

Was he hallucinating?

At a speed that threatened to give everyone in the room whiplash, she turned back to Thanasis. 'The medical team have just declared me fit to travel again, so can I borrow a helicopter to meet Griselda and get the wedding rebooked?'

'Excuse me, miss,' Craig, the Canadian investor, said, 'but you're Thanasis's *fiancée*?'

'Yes, for my sins. I'm so sorry we had to postpone the wedding but I'm sure Thanasis told you all about my relapse. Thank you all so much for not tipping the press off about it—he's been under enough pressure as it is without having to answer constant questions about whether the woman he loves is going to live or die. I really hope you'll all be able to make the rebooked date—I promise we won't make you wait too long. If I had my way we'd sneak off now and marry but my fiancé's a traditionalist and insists on marrying me properly. Anyway, I've taken enough of all your time, so is it okay for me to borrow a helicopter, my love?'

But Thanasis was incapable of speaking. He was watching Lucie bounce around his boardroom, charming and amusing his investors, and was almost completely certain he was dreaming.

He was still almost completely certain he was dreaming when the meeting came to an abrupt halt, files were shuffled together, laptops closed, hands shaken, murmured awkward apologies for all his 'troubles' and then, in what felt like the time it took to blink, the boardroom was empty of everyone but himself and Lucie.

She glided past him.

He caught a waft of her perfume.

She must have pressed the button for all the wall blinds lowered. A lock clicked.

'That's better,' she said happily, perching herself on the table beside him. 'Some privacy.'

He just stared at her.

She slid her bottom over so she was facing him, and reached down to loosen his tie. 'I think the words you're looking for are *thank you*.'

But still he couldn't speak.

'I don't know if you noticed or not, but I've just saved your business.' She smiled and pulled his tie off with a swish. 'You're welcome.'

Suddenly, she slid off the table and onto his lap, straddling him, arms hooked around his neck. The black eyes he'd never believed would look at him again were gazing into his. 'If you ever lie to me again, I'll rip your heart out before I leave you.'

'My heart's already been ripped out,' he said hoarsely.

'Good.' She slid her hands over his throat and opened the top button of his shirt. 'You deserve it.' More buttons were opened in quick succession until she spread his shirt apart and pressed her palm to his chest, right above his pounding heart.

He closed his eyes to the sensation, still struggling to believe what every one of his senses was telling him, that his Aphrodite had appeared before him on her pearl shell and that the warmth starting to unfreeze the coldness of his blood was the warmth from her light.

The warmth of her hands palmed his cheeks. The warmth of her breath danced over his mouth.

He opened his eyes and suddenly she was there, solid, real, his love, shining a love he didn't deserve into him.

She was *here*...

'Did I ever tell you how my parents met?' she said quietly, bringing the tip of her nose to his. 'Mum was a receptionist at Dad's accountancy firm. I think her glamour temporarily blinded him. And that's how I came to be made.

'Dad was Georgios's UK accountant. He did some clever accounting that saved Georgios millions in taxes. To thank him and to celebrate, Georgios insisted on taking the whole firm and their partners out to dinner.'

'He stole your mother from him whilst thanking him?' he whispered, finally bringing his hand to her face.

'If I know my mum, she played an active part in this stealing and, I'm quite sure Dad was secretly glad when she went—I honestly cannot think of two people less compatible.' Her beautiful mouth brushed against his, hands winding round to bury into his hair before she pulled her face back enough to look at him. 'I didn't fit in with either of them or their new families. I tried. I think they tried. But ultimately, my existence has been spent being pulled by fundamentally different parents from fundamentally different worlds. Neither of them wanted to see me as my own person but as an extension of themselves. You, my love, see me exactly as I am and you love me for it, and I fit in with *you*. I belong with you, Thanasis, and if I don't give us the chance we deserve to build something true with all our cards on the table and complete honesty between us, then I will spend the rest of my life regretting it. You are mine and I am yours. The lies you told, they weren't selfish lies. Mum told me those lies for wicked, selfish reasons, because she'd rather destroy her own daughter than lose her lifestyle, but you didn't—you did it for your family. Because you love them. And your guilt over it...' She pressed another gentle kiss to his mouth and sighed. 'I know you felt guilt. I've relived every minute of our time together and I know the lies were eating you up.'

There was a burning sensation in the backs of his eyes. 'I love you, Lucie, and I am so sorry for everything.'

'I know you do and I know you are, and I know in

my heart that we both deserve another chance to find that happiness we were just beginning to create together. When I saw how close you were to losing everything… I couldn't have lived with myself if I hadn't done something. I wanted to save you, just as you've been trying to save everything for your family, because I love *you*.'

She did. He could see it so clearly. A love worth more than all the stars in the sky and all the billions in the world.

He gathered a bunch of soft black curls in his hand and shuddered at how close he'd come to never having touched them again. 'I will never hurt you again. I swear. You are everything to me, Lucie. My whole world.'

Her smile was the sweetest, softest smile in the world. 'I know. And you're my world too.'

'Never leave me.'

'Never.'

And then her mouth fused to his in a kiss that sealed their hearts together for ever.

# EPILOGUE

'WHAT DO YOU THINK?' Lucie asked, closely watching her husband and business partner's reaction. Of all the interior designs she'd created since setting up her own business four years ago, this was the one she was most proud of, the one that made her heart sing nearly as loudly as the man holding her hand so possessively did.

'It is incredible,' he said, awe in his voice as well as his eyes before he cupped her chin and kissed her with the same passion he'd been kissing her for the past six years. 'Your designs just get better and better. Our child will love it,' he murmured when they came up for air, and as he said that, their baby tucked safely in her belly kicked its agreement, hard enough for Thanasis to feel it in his abdomen pressed against hers.

He smiled and then laughed. 'It never feels less than miraculous, does it?'

She beamed, knowing exactly what he meant. The conception of their third child had the same magical feeling to it as her first two pregnancies. 'Never.'

Lucie often felt their entire marriage was built on magic, and thought it was the same magic that had stopped her memories fully returning. She was happy for them to stay lost for ever, but if they ever did return then it didn't matter. She had six years and counting of being loved and cherished to counter it. Six years and counting of utter bliss.

He kissed her again. 'Shall we?'

'Ready when you are.'

'Then let's go.'

They left their unborn child's nursery and quietly checked on their sleeping daughter, Ellie, and their not-quite-sleeping-yet son, Lea, and then, satisfied all was well, left them under the supervision of the nanny and slipped out of the villa.

The golf buggy had been parked out front for them, a huge backpack filled with goodies placed on the back seat.

And then they were off, heading to the mountain to watch the sun set, the route to the summit having long been made safe for a heavily pregnant woman to manage. It was a private journey they never tired of making and a scene they never tired of witnessing, and one they would take together for the rest of their lives.

\* \* \* \* \*